FLETCH

Full name Irwin Maurice Fletcher.
Laid-back man of leisure.
Hard-gunning investigative reporter.

And actress Moxie. She isn't the only love in Fletch's life—
just number one.

Now Fletch is on the story that will break him, make him,
and shake his sanity!

FLETCH

HUSTLING THROUGH
HIS BIGGEST HASSLE YET

Books by Gregory Mcdonald

Running Scared
Fletch
Confess, Fletch
Flynn
Fletch's Fortune
Love Among the Mashed Potatoes
Who Took Toby Rinaldi?
*Fletch and The Widow Bradley

*Published by
WARNER BOOKS

FLETCH AND THE WIDOW BRADLEY

Gregory Mcdonald

WARNER BOOKS

A Warner Communications Company

WARNER BOOKS EDITION

Copyright© 1981 by Gregory Mcdonald
All rights reserved.

Warner Books, Inc., 75 Rockefeller Plaza, New York, N.Y. 10019

Ⓦ A Warner Communications Company

Printed in the United States of America

First Printing: November, 1981

10 9 8 7 6 5 4 3 2 1

FLETCH AND THE WIDOW BRADLEY

1

"Hello," Fletch said. "My name is Armistad."

Behind his desk in his office, the manager of the Park Worth Hotel neither stood nor answered. His eyes telegraphed cold rejection of Fletch's sweater, with no shirt under it, jeans and sneakers. Clearly, in the manager's eyes, Fletch was not up to being a guest in the Park Worth Hotel, or a worthy candidate for a job. Dressed that way, he was not particularly welcome in the hotel lobby.

"Your name is Cavalier?" Fletch asked. A triangular piece of wood on the man's desk said the visage you'd see upon raising your eyes a mite would be that of Jacques Cavalier. Besides the olive wood desk in the managers' office was a large safe, opened, odd stacks of printouts, and a plaster cast of Donatello's *David* perched on a bookshelf full of *National Social Registers*.

The manager twitched his head as if recovering from a flick on the nose. "Yes?"

Fletch sat in one of the two semi-circular backed chairs. He held the wallet in his left hand. "As I said," Fletch said, "my name is Armistad." He pointed with the wallet to the manager's telephone pad. "You might take that down."

"You're not a guest here," the manager said.

"Geoffrey Armistad with a G," Fletch said. "One Three Four Nimble Drive, Santa Monica."

He watched carefully while the manager made the note.

"I'm awfully sorry," the manager said, while dotting the i's. "You do come on like a storm, Geoffrey Armistad with a G, but we're not short of busboys or bellhops, and, if you want kitchen work, you should apply to Chef."

"James Saint E. Crandall," Fletch said.

"Beg pardon?"

"James Crandall. Found his wallet this morning beside my car. Not the usual wallet." Fletch opened it like a paperback book and indicated the plastic shield over the identification insert. "Name says James Saint E. Crandall. Only that. No address. No credit cards, pictures, etc."

Looking at it, Cavalier said, "It's a passport wallet."

"So it is," said Fletch

"And you think this Mister—ah—Crandall is a guest of the Park Worth Hotel?"

"Yes and no. In this little pocket is a key." Fletch dug it out with his fingers and held it up. "The key reads Park Worth Hotel, Room 2019."

"Yes," drawled Jacques Cavalier. "Your object is a reward."

"My object," said Fletch, "is to return the wallet to its owner."

"That seems simple enough," said the manager. "I'll check and make sure Mister Crandall is registered here. If he is, you may leave the wallet with me, and I'll see that he gets it."

"It does seem simple, doesn't it?" Fletch stared over the manager's head at the wall. "You haven't asked what's in the wallet."

Again Cavalier twitched his head. "A passport?"

Again Fletch opened the wallet. "Ten one thousand dollar bills this side..." He fanned the bills on his fingertips. "...Fifteen one thousand dollar bills this side."

"Oh, dear." The manager looked at Fletch with surprised respect. "I'm sure Mister Crandall will be very grateful to you."

"You'd think so, wouldn't you?"

"Indeed I would."

"He's not."

"You mean..." Cavalier cleared his throat. "He refused to negotiate a reward with you."

Fletch leaned forward and put his elbows on the desk.

"I came into your hotel about forty-five minutes ago," Fletch said. "Called Room 2019. A man answered. I asked him if he was James Saint E. Crandall, and he said he was. I told him I'd found his wallet. He seemed pleased. He asked me to wait in the coffee shop. He'd be down in five minutes. I told him I'm wearing a dark blue sweater. I waited in the coffee shop a half hour. Two cups of coffee. Not bad coffee, by the way."

"Thank you."

"He never showed up. After a half hour, I called his room again. No answer. I went up and knocked on his door. No answer."

"You must have missed him. When people say five minutes..."

"When a stranger is waiting to return twenty-five thousand dollars of your money in cash?"

"I don't know."

"Anyway, I checked at your desk. Between the time I first called Crandall and asked at the desk, he had checked out."

"Oh, dear," said the manager. "How very odd."

"Isn't it."

The manager put his hand on the telephone. "I'm calling Mister Smith," said the manager. "He's our hotel detective. We'll see what he can find out."

"Good." Fletch stood up. "While you're doing that, do you mind if I make a phone call? I need to call my boss."

"Of course." The manager indicated another small office. "There's a phone in there."

"Thank you."

"Mister Armistad."

"Yes?"

"Don't you find it amusing our hotel detective's name is Smith?"

Fletch grinned at him.

"People's names frequently amuse me," said Jacques Cavalier.

2

"Hello, Jane. Frank wants to talk to me?"

"Who is this?"

"Gone two days and you don't recognize my voice."

"Oh, hullo, Fletch. How are things up north?"

"Real excitin'. Would you believe I was in a place last night that featured a bald nude dancer?"

"Female or male?"

"What's exciting about a naked bald male?"

"I don't see what baldness has to do with it," Jane said.

"Where's Frank?"

"He didn't mention anything to me about wanting to talk to you."

"The message was waiting for me in the portable terminal this morning. *Call Managing Editor Frank Jaffe immediately. Most urgent.*"

"Oh, you know, everything becomes 'most urgent' with him after a few drinks."

"That's why he's a good managing editor."

"I'll see if he remembers why he wanted you," Jane giggled.

On hold, Fletch was obliged to listen to nine bars of *The Blue Danube Waltz*. A telephone innovation. The business side of the newspaper thought it real classy. The reporters thought it for the birds. Maybe it soothes someone calling up to order advertising space, but someone calls newsside with a hot story, like *The State House is burning down* or *The Governor just ran away with the Senator's wife* and he finds himself dancing a four-square in a telephone booth. It's hard to report temporary sensations and minor perfidies after having just heard violins work through *The Theme From Doctor Zhivago*.

"Hello, Fletch, where are you?" growled Frank Jaffe. Years of treating himself to whiskey had seared the managing editor's vocal chords.

"Good morning, esteemed leader. I'm in the accountant's office at the Park Worth Hotel."

"What're you doing there?"

"Filed from here last night. Incredible front-page story on the race track opening a new clubhouse. You mean it wasn't the first thing you read this morning?"

"Oh, yeah. It was on page 39."

"Can't make caviar from pig's feet."

"Jeez, you didn't stay at the Park Worth, did you?"

"No. Just stopped by to give away twenty-five thousand bucks."

"That's good. Only the publisher gets to stay at the Park Worth. Even he doesn't."

"Your message said I should call you. Urgent, you said."

"Oh, yeah."

Fletch waited. Frank Jaffe said nothing.

"Hello, Frank? You want me to pick up another story while I'm up here? What is it?"

Frank exhaled. "I guess the lead of this story is—you're fired."

Fletch said nothing. He inhaled. Then he said, "What else is new? How's the family?"

"Goofed. You goofed, Fletcher. You goofed big."

"How did I do that?"

"God knows. I don't."

"What did I do?"

"You quoted somebody who's been dead two years."

"I did not."

"Tom Bradley."

"Yeah. The Chairman of Wagnall-Phipps."

"Been dead two years."

"That's nuts. First of all, Frank, I didn't quote Bradley directly—I never spoke to him."

"That's a relief."

"I quoted memos from him."

"Recent memos?"

"Recent. Very recent. I dated them in my story."

"Dead men don't send memos, Fletch."

"Who says he's dead?"

"The executive officers of Wagnall-Phipps. The guy's wife. You make the Tribune look pretty foolish, Fletch. Unreliable, you know?"

Fletch realized he was sitting in the office chair. He didn't remember sitting down.

"Frank, there's got to be some explanation."

"There is. You took a short-cut. You took a big short-cut, Fletcher. Young guys in the newspaper business sometimes do that. This time you got caught."

"Frank, I quoted recent, dated memos initialed 'T.B.' I had them in my hands."

"Must have been some other 'T.B.' Anyway, you did this sloppy, casual story about Wagnall-Phipps, Incorporated, referring throughout to Tom Bradley as the corporation's top dog, quoting him throughout, and he's been dead two years. Frankly, Fletcher, I find this very embarrassing. How is the public supposed to believe our weather reports if we do a thing like that? I mean I know you're not a business reporter, Fletch. You never should have been assigned this story. But a good reporter should be able to cover anything."

Fletch put the wallet on the desk and rubbed his left hand on his thigh, removing the sweat.

"Let's talk about it as a suspension, Fletch. You've done some good work. You're young yet."

"How long a suspension?"

"Three months?" The managing editor sounded like he was trying the idea out on Fletch.

"Three months. Frank, I can't survive three months. I've got alimony to pay. Car payments. I haven't got a dime."

"Maybe you should go get another job. Maybe suspension isn't such a good idea. I haven't heard from the publisher yet. He probably won't like the idea of just suspending you."

"Jeez, Frank. This is terrible."

"Sure is. Everyone around here is laughing at you. It's going to be hard to live a story like this down."

"Frank. I feel innocent. You know what I mean?"

"Joan of Arc you're not."

"At least give me a chance to check my sources."

"Like who?" Frank Jaffe chuckled. "Saint Peter? You get him on the line, I want to know."

"Okay, Frank. Am I suspended, or fired, or what?"

"Let me try out suspension and see how it flies. The publisher's in Santa Fe with his wife. The financial editor wants your head on a plate. You're probably fired. Call me next week."

"Thanks, Frank."

"Hey, Fletch, want me to send you your paycheck? Janey can stick it in the mail to you."

"No, thanks."

"I just thought coming into the office would be sort of embarrassing for you."

"No, thanks. I'll come in."

"No one ever said you're short of guts, Fletch. Well, if you do come in to the office, wear your football helmet and your steel jock-strap."

3

"Wagnall-Phipps. Good morning."

"Mister Charles Blaine, please."

Fletch succeeded in keeping his voice steady. Still in the accounting office of The Park Worth Hotel he had dialed Long-distance Information and then called Wagnall-Phipps using his newspaper's telephone credit card. With his fingers he picked his sweater away from his sweaty skin.

"Mister Blaine's office."

"Is he there?"

"I'm sorry, Mister Blaine has left for the day."

Fletch glanced at his watch. "It's only eleven thirty in the morning."

"I know," the secretary said. "Mister Blaine has the flu."

"It's terribly important I talk with him. This is Jay Russell. I'm on a charity committee with Mister Blaine—the Committee to Preserve Antique Silver Clouds."

There was a long pause. "Silver clouds?" the secretary asked. "How do you preserve them?"

"They're a kind of car," Fletch said. "A kind of Rolls Royce."

"Oh," said the secretary. "For a minute there I thought you were really on to something."

"May I have Mister Blaine's home phone number?"

"No, I'm sorry. That's against company policy."

"This is terribly important."

"So's company policy. At least to me. You wouldn't want to get me fired."

"I wouldn't want to get anybody fired. Believe me. Mister Blaine will be very glad to hear from me. I can assure you there will be no recriminations if you give me his number."

"I know there won't be any recriminations—if I don't give it to you at all."

Fletch hung up.

His hand still on the receiver, Fletch said, "Damn, damn, damn!"

He checked his own billfold. He had two twenties, a ten, a five, and two one dollar bills, plus a blank check. He tried to remember whether he had a balance in his checking account of one hundred and twenty dollars, or if that had been the month before, or even the month before that. Sometime he had had a balance of one hundred and twenty dollars. At most he had less than two hundred dollars in cash, one paycheck due, and no job.

He picked up the phone and dialed a local number. He rang five times.

"Hello?" Moxie's voice said sleepily.

"Are you just waking up?"

"I don't know. What are you doing on the phone? Why aren't you in bed beside me?"

"Always a good question."

"Where are you?"

"Park Worth Hotel."

"Why?"

"I dunno. I went out to the car to check the computer terminal for messages. I found a wallet. That led me to the Park Worth Hotel. It's a long story."

"It's always a long story with you, Fletch."

"Some days you shouldn't get up in the morning."

"Most days you shouldn't get up in the morning. Is something wrong with you, Fletch?"

"Ha—ha, he said cheerily, what could be wrong?"

"What's wrong?"

"Just one or two minor things. I'll explain later. Do you still want to drive down the coast with me today?"

"Yeah. What time do you have to be back in the office?"

"In about three months."

"What?"

"We've got plenty of time. Why don't you get up, pack, make us a picnic lunch, a picnic supper, a picnic breakfast—"

"Can't we stop along the way?"

"Not to eat."

"All I've got is a jar of peanut butter. I've been letting the supplies run down."

"Bring the whole jar. I'll pick up the bread and orange juice."

"Traveling with you sounds like a real treat."

"Fifth class all the way. I'll be by in about an hour."

"An hour and a half."

"It doesn't take that long to pack a jar of peanut butter."

"It does when I lost the top of the jar six weeks ago."

"How can you lose the top of a peanut butter jar?"

"I *think* I mistook it for an elephant, and you know those elephants—"

"Yeah," said Fletch. "Always getting lost. Don't be too long. Thought we'd stop on the way down, beach I know, for a swim."

"You have that much free time?"

"I have time," said Fletch. "And it's all free."

4

"I'm sorry," Fletch said. "I didn't expect my phone call to take that much time."

Jacques Cavalier was sitting behind his olive wood desk, but in the chair where Fletch had been sitting was a short, middle-aged man with an angelic face. He was looking at Fletch with curiosity, and Cavalier was looking at Fletch with concern.

"Are you all right, Mister Armistad?" Cavalier asked.

"Sure, sure," Fletch said. "Just hot in that other room."

"Mister Armistad," Cavalier insisted. "You're pale. Have you had a shock?"

"Oh, that," Fletch said easily. "My boss just told me that a friend.. of mine has been fired."

"How very distressing," said Cavalier. "Tell me, Mister Armistad: what do you do for a living?"

"I park cars."

"A humble enough job." Cavalier smiled. "Why was your friend fired?"

"He tried to park two cars in the same space. Almost succeeded. Chuck never did have a very good memory."

"This is Mister Smith, our house detective." Cavalier consulted his note pad. "Mister Geoffrey with a G. Armistad—our honest friend who parks cars for a living."

"Hiya," said the middle-aged man with the angelic face.

Fletch sat in the free chair.

"I've repeated to Mister Smith your remarkable story, Mister Armistad. He is, you might say, incredulous."

"Lemme see the wallet," Smith said.

Fletch handed it to him. The detective counted the twenty five bills individually.

"Okay." Smith placed the wallet on the desk. "I've checked. A man giving his name as James St. E. Crandall checked into the hotel at four P.M. three days ago. He checked out this morning just before Jacques called me. Paid cash." Smith read from the itemized bill in his hands. "He had room service for breakfast for one, for both mornings he was here. Yesterday he had a pair of trousers pressed. The night he arrived he had one beer brought to his room about ten-thirty, so we can guess he retired early. He had no other bar-bill or restaurant charges in the hotel. He made six local calls, all in all, and no long-distance calls. He gave as his address 47907 Courier Drive, Wramrud. He put down nothing on the line for Company Name, Business Affiliation."

Fletch had signalled Cavalier for a piece of paper and pen and was writing down the address.

"I've checked his room," Smith continued. "Nothing out of the ordinary. Usual wrinkled sheets and towels."

"He was known to your people at the Reception Desk?"

Smith said, "I asked the cashier, who checked Crandall out, for a description. He said the guy was either fifty and balding or seventy and stooped. I guess two people were checking out at the same time."

"But someone on your Reception Desk knew him."

"Why do you say that?" Smith asked.

"You said Crandall paid cash when he left. Reception desks like to run a credit card when a person checks in—don't they?"

Smith glanced at Cavalier.

"This is a first class hotel, Mister Armistad."

"You don't have first class crooks?"

"We try to bother our guests as little as possible. Of course, sometimes we get stuck..." Cavalier raised his hands and shrugged. "...but we consider it worth it not to distrust everybody. Our guests trust us; we should trust them."

Fletch asked, "How many people pay their hotel bills in cash?"

"A good many," said Cavalier. "At this hotel. We still have the little old ladies in tennis shoes, you know—and they're not all little old ladies— who do not put themselves in the way of being mugged by either someone in the street, or, a credit card company."

"We have other guests who pay cash, too."

Smith chuckled at Crandall. "Every hotel has those—here on private business, we call it."

"Breakfast for one," Fletch said. "Two days running. Doesn't sound like Crandall was sharing his room with anyone."

"Doesn't necessarily mean anything," Smith said. "There are lots of other hours in a day."

"Yeah, but what percentage of your guests pay in cash?"

"About ten percent," said Cavalier.

"More like fifteen," said Smith

"Mister Smith is obliged to think on the seamier side of things," Cavalier said.

"So there was nothing really unusual about this guest, James St. E. Crandall."

"Yeah," laughed Smith. "He ducked out on somebody trying to return twenty-five thousand dollars cash to him. That's a new experience for us."

Cavalier had been studying Fletch. "Hope you don't mind my saying, Mister Armistad, but you're not my idea of a parking lot attendant."

"Have you known many parking lot attendants?"

Cavalier smirked. "Not intimately."

Taking the wallet off the desk, Fletch stood up. "Thank you both for your help," he said.

Cavalier asked, "You're taking the wallet?"

"What else?"

"Well, I don't know." Cavalier looked at Smith. "I'm sure I don't know what to do. This isn't a simple matter of Lost and Found. I suppose I had been thinking the next thing we would do would be to notify the police."

"Oh, I'm going to the police," said Fletch.

"Sure," Smith said.

"I came here, didn't I?"

"Yes, you did come here." Cavalier ran his middle finger over his creased brow. "And you did find the money. And not on hotel premises..you say."

"Not within twenty blocks of here."

"And the man did run out on you...are you sure you called the right room?"

"No," said Fletch. "Everybody gets a wrong number once in a while. But the hotel guest I spoke to didn't seem surprised when I told him he'd lost a wallet."

Fletch put the wallet in the back pocket of his jeans.

"I really don't know," Cavalier said. "I suppose we'll have to notify the police, in any case." He smiled at Fletch. "Just to protect ourselves, you understand."

"A kid walks in with twenty-five thousand dollars," muttered Smith, "and walks out with twenty-five thousand dollars."

"I expect you to call the police," Fletch said. "I gave you my name, didn't I?" He pointed at the pad on Cavalier's desk. "And my address?"

"Yes, you did, Mister Armistad," said Jacques Cavalier. "Indeed you did."

5

"A jar of peanut butter, a loaf of bread, a jug of orange juice, and thou," Fletch said.

Bellies on the sand, head to head, at only a slight angle to each other, they were still wet from their swim. They were alone in the cove.

"Pretty romantic," said Moxie.

"Pretty romantic."

"Not very." The late afternoon sun sparkled in the dots of salt water on her arms, her back, her legs. "Peanut butter, bread and orange juice."

"And thou."

"And wow. Not chopped carrots and strained beans, but it still doesn't cut the mustard romantically, Fletch." Moxie rose up enough to brush sand off her bare breast, then settled her cheek against her forearm and sighed. "Not very romantic days, these."

"You don't think so?"

"Romance is gone from life. A thing of the past."

"Sob."

"Gone with crinolines and cramps."

"I thought I was pretty romantic."

"Sure. Pick me up at one thirty, ignore the reservation for two I made at the Cafe Mondrian, drive like a bobsled team captain to this abandoned beach down here, passing up several good places to stop for lunch—"

"You hungry?"

"—tumble me around in the surf like a—like a..."

"Like a what?"

"Like an equal." She wriggled forward on her elbows and kissed him on the cheek. "Do it in the sand without even a blanket, a towel, anything."

"Fair's fair. We did it on our sides."

"Not very romantic." Moxie blew in his face.

"Romance was an idea created by the manufacturers of wine and candle sticks."

"And smelling salts."

She licked his cheek.

"What could be more romantic than peanut butter and orange juice? That's protein and Vitamin C you're scoffing at, girl. Very energizing foodstuffs, you know."

"You getting energetic again, Fletcher?"

"Sure," he said. "It's been a whole five minutes."

They had examined the hillsides above them the first time. There was only one house overlooking the cove, and that was pretty far back. Its main plate-glass window looked blind.

They were sitting on the sand, washing peanut butter sandwiches down with orange juice.

"So?" Moxie said.

"So I took the twenty-five thousand dollars..." He took the orange juice carton from her and drank. "What do you want to know?"

"Last night, if I remember correctly, you were full of self-importance and duty and went on and on about getting back to the newspaper today in time to work the night shift and if I wanted a ride with you I had to be up and packed and ready to go before I woke up..."

"Self-importance?"

"Damned near pomposity."

"You're not famous for getting up early in the morning, Moxie."

"I'm not famous for anything. Yet. Sleeping late was the first thing I learned in Drama School."

"Really?"

"Yeah. All the classes were in the afternoon."

"You theater people have to be different."

"I don't know what time the night shift on a newspaper starts, Fletch, but that red frog crapping on the ocean over there is the setting sun. And I figure we're a good seven hours drive from your precious newspaper."

"I'm a changed man."

"What changed you?"

"I got fired."

Fletch watched the shallow crease in her stomach breathe in and out a few times. She said, "Oh." Then she said, "Hey." She resumed chewing. "You liked that job."

"It gave paychecks, too."

"You can get a job on another newspaper. Can't you?"

"I really doubt it."

"What happened?"

"Long story. Sort of complicated."

"Make it simple. If I don't understand first time 'round, I can ask questions. Right?"

"Well, I was assigned to do an unimportant story on an unimportant business company and I guess I got sold a big, fat lie." Fletch spoke rapidly. "My main source was a guy named Blaine. Charles Blaine. Vice-president and treasurer. He gave me a file of memos back and forth between him and the Chairman of the company, a guy named Tom Bradley, and said I could quote from them. So I did."

"So what went wrong?"

"Tom Bradley died two years ago."

"Died?"

"Died."

"Died dead?"

"Deader than romance."

"You quoted a dead man?"

"Very accurately."

Moxie giggled. "Jeez, that's pretty good, Fletch."

"I could have done worse," Fletch said. "I suppose I could have quoted somebody who'd never existed."

"I'm sorry." Moxie rubbed her nose.

"What for?"

"For laughing."

"It's funny. Wake me in the morning."

"Were these recent memos you quoted? They couldn't have been."

"They were recently dated memos. I put their dates in the story I wrote."

"I don't get it."

"That makes at least two of us."

Her eyes went back and forth over the sea. They were purple flecked with yellow in the setting sun. "Was it some kind of a mean joke?"

"Pretty mean. I guess someone meant to do mischief."

"Who? Why?"

"Blaine, I guess. He had to know what he was doing, giving me memos from a dead man. Maybe he's crazy."

"Have you gone back to him? Tried to get in touch with him?"

"Tried this morning. He'd left his office. Sick with the flu."

"No." Moxie shook her head. "That's too crazy. No one would do a thing like that. As a joke."

"Not a joke," Fletch said. "Maybe you've heard that some American businesses are waging a clever campaign to get back at the press. Make the newspapers and television look silly."

"How would I have heard that?"

"It's a growing thing. They say there are too many liberals in the press. Anti-business liberals."

"Are there?"

"Probably. More specifically, the *News-Trib* worked this particular corporation, Wagnall-Phipps, over pretty good two or three years ago."

"For what?"

"Influence buying. Wining and dining congressmen, mayors and others on the public payroll in a position to buy shovels and toothpicks from Wagnall-Phipps."

"Did you write those stories?"

"I wasn't even working for the *News-Trib* then. I was in Chicago."

"You're the fall guy."

"My own fault. I didn't care about this Wagnall-Phipps story. I was working on that football story, you know, at the same time. I cared a lot more about that story. I scanned the clips on Wagnall-Phipps, saw the key question was whether the corporation still owned that big ski house in Aspen they used to lend to congressmen and their families, and went off to interview Blaine. I remember I had a hard time staying awake listening to him. He finally put me in an office by myself and let me take notes from this sheaf of memos."

"So you don't have the memos, or copies of the memos yourself."

"No. I don't. Simple, stupid, unimportant story I didn't even think the newspaper would print, it was so boring. Who cares about Wagnall-Phipps?"

"I guess Wagnall-Phipps does."

"I was only assigned the story 'cause the reporter originally assigned to it, Tom Jeffries, broke his back hang-gliding."

"That's terrible."

"That is terrible. I'm no business writer. Shit, I don't even know how to read stock tables. I'd never heard of Wagnall-Phipps before."

"But why dump on you?"

"Nothing personal. They weren't dumping on me. They were making the newspaper look silly. They did a pretty good job."

"They took advantage of your ignorance."

"Sure. Along comes bushy-tailed Peter Rabbit

with his mouth open and they feed him loaded carrots. They refer to the Chairman of their board, Thomas Bradley, show me memos from him, and I write down, *In a memo dated April 16, Chairman of the Board, Thomas Bradley, directed etc., etc.* I mean, wouldn't you believe the Vice-president and treasurer of a corporation regarding who was the Chairman of the company?"

Moxie shook her head. "Poor Peter Rabbit."

"Poor Peter Rabbit nothin'. He's a dope."

"So you're fired."

"Well, the managing editor is breaking it to me gently. He's talking about a three-months suspension, but that's only so he can insist later he tried to save my job."

"No chance?"

"I wouldn't hire me. Would you?"

"More orange juice? There's another quart."

"We'll need it in the morning."

"So what were you doing this morning at the Park Worth Hotel?"

"Oh, that's another story. We've got to stop by and see a guy about it in Wramrud tomorrow. Found his wallet."

"Fletch, I'm cold. If you glance westward, you'll notice even the sun has found a better place to go."

Fletch said, "I'll build a fire."

She stared at him. "You mean to spend the night here?"

"Sure. Romantic."

"On the beach?"

"How much money you got on you, Moxie?"

"I don't know. Maybe fifty dollars."

"I thought so. You begin rehearsing for the new play Monday. When do you get your first paycheck?"

"End of next week."

"So you've got fifty bucks to live off for a week and I've got about the same amount to live off for the rest of my life. Dig?"

"Credit cards, Fletch. You used one last night. At dinner. Even I've got a credit card."

"I've got a sleeping bag in the car."

"You're getting me to spend the night on the beach with you."

"I told you. I'm very romantic." Standing, Fletch brushed the sand off his skin.

"And I told you romance is dead."

"That's just wishful thinking," Fletch said. "I'll get the sleeping bag."

6

"Trying to find my uncle," Fletch said.

It had taken the creaky old policeman a long moment to stand up from his padded swivel chair and walk across the main room of the Wramrud Police Station to the counter. There was a hearing aid in his left ear.

"His name is James Crandall." Fletch spoke slowly and distinctly.

"Live here in town?"

"Supposed to."

"What do you mean 'supposed to'? Nobody's 'supposed to' live anywhere. Haven't you heard this is a free country?"

"My mother gave me this address." Fletch handed the policeman the piece of note paper he'd had from Jacques Cavalier's desk.

"I can't find Courier Drive," Fletch said.

"47907 Courier Drive, Wramrud," the old policeman read aloud.

"The man in the drugstore doesn't seem to know where it is."

The policeman looked at Fletch sharply. "Bob doesn't know where it is?"

"I guess not."

"This Crandall fellow. He your mother's brother?"

"Yes," said Fletch.

"You know you have sand on your face?"

Fletch brushed his face with his hand.

"Why do you have sand on your face?"

Fletch shrugged. "I was playing in a sandbox."

"You ought to shave before you see your uncle."

"Yeah. I guess I should."

The policeman looked again at the piece of paper in his hand. "Bob don't know where Courier Drive, Wramrud, is because there is no Courier Drive, Wramrud."

"There isn't?"

"Your mother lie to you often, son?"

"First time ever."

"Far as you know. Nope. No Courier Drive. Fact is, we don't have anything called a Drive around here. Lots of roads and streets but nothing as fancy as a Drive."

"You have any street like Courier?"

"How do we know?"

"I mean, a street that sounds like Courier, or might look like Courier written out."

The man's rheumy eyes gazed through the plate glass window. "Century Street. Cold Water

36

Road. We don't have any address numbers that run that high, either. Forty-seven thousand something. We only got nineteen hundred households this whole town."

"You know a man named Crandall?"

"You mean, your uncle?"

"Yes."

"Nope. Man named Cranshaw, not your uncle."

Fletch smiled. "How do you know?"

" 'Cause I'm Cranshaw and my sister don't lie."

"Okay," Fletch said. "I give up. You've never heard of a man named Crandall in this town."

"Nope. And we're the only town named Wramrud I ever heard of, too. You ever heard of another town named Wramrud?"

"No."

The policeman's eyes were inspecting Fletch's neck and sweater. "You got sand all over you, boy. You want a shower?"

"What?"

"You want to take a shower? Shave?"

"Where?"

"Back in the lock-ups. I can give you a fresh razor."

"Mighty nice of you."

"Well, seems to me you have a long way to go to find your uncle." The policeman lifted a section of the counter to let Fletch through. "Any boy whose mother tells whoppers like your's—ain't no tellin' where you might end up."

Fletch followed the policeman toward the door to the jail cells.

"Why do you suppose your mother would tell

you a lie like that?" the old policeman asked. "Do you suppose you have an uncle at all? 'pect she told you he's rich..."

"Your hair is wet," Moxie said. She was waiting by the car. "And you shaved."

"I got cleaned up."

"Where?"

"In the jailhouse. Want a shower? Nice old policeman."

"How'd it smell?"

"Terrible."

"No, thanks. I'd rather shower at your apartment."

Fletch started the car and took the road back toward the highway. "There is no James St. E. Crandall in Wramrud. Never has been."

Moxie rubbed her back against the back of the car seat and then scratched her elbow. "I am itchy. We are going straight to your apartment, aren't we?"

"No."

"Oh, lord. Fletch, I can understand your natural reluctance to get back to the city—we can hear the general laughter from here—but I do want a proper meal and a proper shower."

"Thought we'd stop at Frank Jaffe's house first."

"Who's he? Does he exist, or did he die?"

"He's my managing editor. My ex-managing editor."

"You think you can find his house?"

"I know where he lives. We go right by it."

"Boy, Fletch. Someone told me you're a great

reporter. Can't even find a person in a little town like Wramrud, or wherever we just were."

"Who told you I'm a great reporter?"

"You did."

Coming onto the freeway, Fletch stepped on the accelerator, hard. "Guess I was wrong."

7

"My God." Moxie stood on the front walk looking at the lit facade of the house. It was an English Tudor-styled house with established shrubs. "This is where the managing editor of the *News-Tribune* lives?"

"Yeah."

"I'll bet those wooden beams are fake."

Fletch was ringing the doorbell.

"Moxie? Where are you going?"

Clara Snow opened the door. She had a half-empty martini glass in her hand.

"Fletch!"

"Evening, Clara. Didn't expect to find you here."

Clara did not smile. "Didn't know you were expected, Fletcher."

"You know, when Frank gives an at-home party for his employees—"

"This is not an at-home party."

"Well, Frank must be home, and you're at home with him, and you are an employee..."

"Come in, Fletch."

"Wait a minute. I have a friend."

Fletch looked along the side of the house, to the right, where Moxie was coming out of the established shrubbery.

"How do you do?" she said, shaking hands with Clara. "So nice to meet you, Mrs. Jaffe."

"This isn't Mrs. Jaffe," said Fletch.

Closing the door behind them, Clara said, "Fletch, you've got some balls."

"I've got Moxie," Fletch said.

Frank was in the livingroom, dressed in a ski sweater. He was putting another log on the fire. Fletch could feel the air-conditioning in the house was on.

"Evening, Frank," he said.

Frank looked over his glasses at Fletch. "You're fired, Fletcher. If you weren't before, you certainly are now."

"Why?"

"Because it's Friday night and this is my home and fired employees aren't supposed to come to their boss' home uninvited on Friday nights. Or ever. It just isn't polite."

"Even if I'm in pursuit of a story?"

"What story?"

"That's what you're going to tell me."

Frank was staring at Moxie. "You're a beautiful girl," he said.

"Thank you, sir," Moxie said prettily.

"Really beautiful."

Clara Snow moved around the coffee table and sat on the divan.

"This is Moxie Mooney," Fletch said. "She's an actress. Starting rehearsals Monday for a play at the Colloquial Theater."

"As long as you're here," Frank said, "you might as well have a drink. Least I haven't lost my manners."

"Thanks, Frank. Where's Betty?"

Standing over the bar table, pouring two more martinis and freshening his own glass, Frank said, "My wife is in San Francisco. For a weekend of shopping and seeing her brother's family. Any other questions, Fletch?"

"Sure." Fletch looked at Clara Snow.

Frank said, "Clara is here for dinner with me and to talk over some editorial matters."

"Talking over editorial matters with a state house reporter. I see."

Clara had been cooking editor until letters of complaint had become overwhelming. Her recipes were making people sick. The Clara Snow Flu was a city room joke. Reporters with heavy hangovers would call up to say they were too sick to work because they had eaten something Clara Snow had recommended. Everyone had been perplexed as to how and why Clara had been transferred from that job to the highly prestigious job of state house reporter.

"Political matters," Frank said. "Now, do you want a drink, Fletcher, or do you want me to kick your ass through the front door without opening it?"

Fletch sat on the divan facing Clara. "Sure,

Frank. I like martinis. Sorry to interrupt your meeting with Clara."

Frank handed Moxie a martini and put Fletch's on the coffee table. "Sit down, sit down," he said to Moxie. "Might as well make yourself at home. Fletch has."

Moxie sat beside Fletch, and Frank sat in a chair with his fresh drink.

"What's the name of the play you're in?" Frank asked Moxie.

"*In Love*, sort of a romantic comedy."

"Didn't know they produced romantic comedies anymore," Frank said. "I'd like to see one."

"You're the ingenue?" Clara asked. At thirty, Clara had blossomed into full womanhood.

"Yes," Moxie answered. "It's a comedy about rape."

"Hilarious," Clara said, "I'm sure."

"Not rape, really," said Moxie. "You see, it's about this young girl who was very strictly brought up and every time her young husband touches her, she thinks she's being raped. So every time he tries to make love to her, she has him arrested. You see?"

"Could be amusing, I suppose," Frank Jaffe said.

"But husbands can rape wives," Fletch said.

"The funny thing is," said Moxie, looking into her martini glass, "the young couple really do love each other. They're just terribly confused, you know, regarding their rights to each other, and themselves."

"A lawyer in every bedroom," Frank said. "That's what we need."

"Wagnall-Phipps," Fletch said.

Frank looked at him. "What?"

"Can't say you're not talking business tonight, Frank. We interrupted a business meeting between you and Clara."

"I'm willing to talk newspaper business anytime," Frank said. "I'm just not sure how willing I am to talk over Wagnall-Phipps with you. A goof's a goof, Fletch. Hard to take, but there you are."

"A story's a story, Frank."

"Don't get you."

"The Vice-president and treasurer of Wagnall-Phipps refers to the chairman of his company as Thomas Bradley, shows me memos from him— recent memos—and someone else tells you that Thomas Bradley is dead. I need some facts."

"You needed some facts before you wrote the story," Clara said.

"Okay." Frank looked from one employee to the other. "I read the early edition here at my breakfast table per usual. I only scanned your story, wondering who in heck had assigned you to a business news story. You with your cut-off blue jeans and bare feet—"

"Barefoot boy with cheek," Clara said softly.

"You've never struck me as a business news writer," Frank said, smiling at Fletch.

"Tom Jeffries got hurt hang-gliding."

"I know. So I go into the office and there's a call waiting for me from an Enid Bradley. She says she's the chairperson of Wagnall-Phipps and has been since her husband died. While I'm listening to her mild voice on the phone, I open the newspaper to your story, scan it again and see that you've quoted her husband, Thomas Bradley, throughout. Recent quotes."

"From memos," Fletch said.

"You have copies of any of those memos?" Frank asked.

"No."

"So I called Jack Carradine, the business news editor, who had just returned from a trip to New York—"

"I know Jack's the business news editor," Fletch said.

"—and he doesn't seem sure whether Bradley's dead or alive. Apparently Wagnall-Phipps isn't that important a company. He calls the president of Wagnall-Phipps and is told the same thing—Bradley's dead. Didn't I tell you all this on the phone?"

"No. You didn't tell me Mrs. Bradley herself called you, or that she is now chairperson of Wagnall-Phipps, and you said you had confirmation from 'executive officers' of Wagnall-Phipps, not just one guy—the president."

Clara sighed and looked sideways at Frank.

Frank said, "Dead's dead."

Moxie said, "It's none of my business, of course, but I think this Wagnall-Phipps company played a trick on Fletch. The *News-Tribune* did an exposé on Wagnall-Phipps a couple of years ago—"

"People play tricks on reporters all the time," Frank said. "No one ever tells the exact truth. People always say to a reporter what serves their own interest best. Good reporters know this and just don't get caught."

"Fletch got caught," said Clara. "And that's the end of the story."

"Frank, will you keep me on salary until I get this thing figured out?"

"What's to figure?" asked Frank. "Mrs. Phipps —I mean, Mrs. Bradley said she didn't want her children reading in the newspaper things her husband recently said. Can you blame her? She said they're just getting over the death now."

Fletch shook his head. "There's something wrong, Frank."

"Sure there is." Clara walked to the bar to pour herself a new drink. "Irwin Maurice Fletcher and his sloppy reporting. That's what's wrong."

Frank leaned forward, elbow on his knees. "Look, Fletch. Carradine called Mrs. Wagnall—I mean, Mrs. Bradley back and made all smooth. He even went to the house last night and spent an hour talking to the Bradley kids, saying newspapers sometimes make mistakes. Nobody's suing us. But the story that we quoted a dead man is all over the country now, and it hurts, Fletch. It hurts the paper. Our publisher picked it up out in Santa Fe and called me. I was going to wait until he got back."

"What'd he say?" asked Fletch.

Frank settled back in his chair. "I asked for a suspension. Honest, I did, Fletch."

"And he said no?"

"What do you think?"

"He said no." Fletch stood up.

"You didn't drink your drink," Frank said.

"I drank mine," Moxie said.

Frank smiled at her. "Anything as gorgeous as you are shouldn't drink."

Clara turned slowly from the bar and stared at him.

"Just one more question, Frank," Fletch said.

"What?"

"Is Clara cooking dinner for you?"

"Yes. Why?"

"I'll call the office," Fletch said, "and tell Janey you won't be in Monday."

8

"You supposed to be here?" The *News-Tribune*'s assistant librarian stood in the doorway glaring at Fletch.

It was a quarter to eight Saturday morning.

Looking up from the microfilm consol, Fletch said, "I can be."

"I heard this newspaper no longer requires your services."

"I heard that, too."

"So you should no longer have access to this newspaper's excellent services. Such as our microfilm library."

Fletch turned the consol off and gathered up his note papers. "Come on, Jack. Gimme a break."

"Wait a minute." The barrel-chested man stepped in front of Fletch and held out his hand. "Let me see what you're takin' out of here."

"Just some notes."

"On what? Come on, I want to see."

Fletch handed Jack his notes and waited while he scanned them.

"James Saint Edward Crandall. Address Newtowne. Who's he?"

"I don't know."

Jack's eyes flickered high-beam at Fletch.

"Charles Blaine. Address Bel Monte. You quoted him in that marvelous story of yours Wednesday. Everyone around here has given that story another real close read—as you might expect."

"I expect."

"Thomas Bradley. Chairman of the Board, Wagnall-Phipps. Married Enid Riordan. Two children. Address Southworth. You quoted him in that story too, didn't you?" He grinned at Fletch. "You don't give up easy, do you?"

"Should I?"

Jack handed Fletch back his notes. "I guess everyone has a right to try to save his own ass—even when his ass has already been whipped."

"May I use your phone, Jack?"

"Get out of here now and I won't have you arrested for trespassing."

"Okay, okay." At the door, Fletch turned and said, "Jack?"

"I'm still seeing you. Trespasser."

"Want to know something interesting?"

"Yeah. Who's going to win the third race at Hialeah this afternoon? Tell me so I can make points with Osborne. Knowing you you'll probably say Trigger."

"No obit."

"Trigger had a nice obit. Just before Roy Rogers had him stuffed."

"Yeah." Fletch pointed to the consol. "But there is no obit for Tom Bradley in there."

"Lots of people die we don't print the obit. We're not properly notified. Bradley was no captain of American industry."

"I just find it interesting."

"Write a nice story about how they stuffed Tom Bradley. Only get the competition to print it this time, willya, Fletch?"

Standing over his own desk in the city room, Fletch dialed his own home number. The phone rang seven times.

Nearby, drinking coffee, sat four reporters and one photographer. They were gathered around Al's desk. Leaning back in his chair, Al had his feet on his desk. Al was a middle-aged reporter who complained of feet trouble and back problems and always managed to be the last one sent out on assignment. Mostly he held court, passed rumor and gossip in the city room.

They had grinned broadly at each other when Fletch had entered the city room from the library.

"Mornin', Irwin," Al sang to Fletch. "Don't remember ever seeing you here this early on a Saturday morning before. What happened? You get thrown out of bed, too?"

"Telephone," Moxie said. "I mean, hello?"

"Good morning, sunshine," Fletch turned his back on the reporters.

"Fletch? Why are you always waking me up in the morning?"

"Because that's the time of day people get up. Bounce out of bed. Do their breathing exercises."

"I didn't sleep well last night."

"You were asleep when I left."

Moxie yawned into the phone. "I lay awake a long time after you went to sleep. Thinking about the play. Watching you sleep. Thinking about how much trouble you're in. I mean, Fletch, you're ruined."

"Down but not out, old thing."

"Those people last night, your managing editor, Frank, and that dreadful woman, what's her name—"

"Clara Snow."

"They wouldn't have let you into the house if I hadn't been there. Frank would have thrown you through the door and that Clara person would have stomped on your head with a high-heeled shoe."

"If that's a question, the answer is: yes—I was using you. Do you object?"

" 'Course not."

"Frank has an eye for beauty. His left one, I think."

"By the way, I was right."

" 'Bout what?"

"You know those wooden beams on the outside of his house? They're plastic."

"No! And here he's supposed to be some kind of a tastemaker. Stylesetter. Trendspotter. Managing editor."

"Some kind of synthetic. A hollow synthetic at that. I knocked against them."

"You have the makings of a reporter, Moxie. Wish I had."

"Courage, Fletch."

"Listen, I have to do a lot of driving around today. Want to come?"

"Where?"

"No place interesting. The suburbs. Got to see people."

"Just spent two days in a car with you. Two days in a car and one night on a beach. Six peanut butter sandwiches, three quarts of orange juice, and home to your apartment for wet spaghetti made wetter by a can of tomato soup."

"Candlelit dinner."

"Yeah. Thanks for dragging out your hurricane lamp. Real romantic. Like being on a sinking ship. At least I got a shower. Had a hell of a time not scratching myself at Frank's house."

"You did very well. Hardly twitched."

"Wasn't going to scratch in front of that Clara person."

"You don't want to come with me?"

"No. I'll go back to sleep for another few minutes. Should study the playscript."

"I might not be back until late."

"I'll take a walk, if I get bored."

"Right. Give the neighborhood a treat. See you."

"Hey. Is there any food in this house?"

"See you."

Fletch turned around and found the group of reporters watching him. Naturally, they had been trying to listen.

"Just trying to locate a *hari-kiri* sword," Fletch said. "With a booklet of instructions as to how to use it."

"Hey, Fletch?" Al drawled.

"Yes, Al?"

"Do me a favor, Fletch?"

"Sure, Al. Anything, for you. Want me to use my influence with Frank? Get you a raise?"

"I wish you'd interview someone for me." Al winked at the men sitting around his desk.

"Sure, Al. Who?"

"Dwight Eisenhower. I think ol' Ike still might have a few things to say."

"Sure, Al. I'll do it before lunch."

"Napoleon?" the photographer asked.

"Did him last month," Fletch said. "Thanks for reading the *News-Tribune*."

"Did you get any good hard quotes out of Napoleon?" Al asked.

"He really opened up on Josephine."

"Yeah? What did he say about Josephine?"

"Said she wore hair curlers in bed. That's why he spent so much time in the field."

"Really, Fletch," said a reporter named Terry. "You could get a job with one of those spooky magazines. You know? 'What Abraham Lincoln Said To Me.' That sort of thing."

"Or maybe a morticians' trade paper," the photographer said. "You could be their Consumer Affairs Columnist."

"Keep laughin', guys."

"Or you could quote Thomas Bradley again," said an old reporter, who was not smiling.

Fletch glanced at the big wall clock. "Guess I better hurry up, if I'm going to make that interview with *The New York Times*. Shouldn't keep 'em waiting too long. They want a new managing editor, you know."

"Geè, no, Fletch. We didn't hear that," said the photographer.

Terry said, "Ernie Pyle should get the job. Maybe H.L. Mencken."

Al called after Fletch, as Fletch was leaving the city room. "Aren't you cleaning out your desk?"

"Hell, no," Fletch said. "I'll be back."

"Yeah," the unsmiling reporter said. "Maybe in your next life."

9

"God, I hate this," Tom Jeffries said. On a high metal bed on wheels, on which he was lying on his stomach in the tiny patio behind his house, he was dressed only in shorts and, from his waist to his head, plaster casts and metal braces. His friend, Tina, was sitting on a stool spooning scrambled egg into his mouth. She was dressed in a light, loose dress. "Everything you eat sticks in your throat. Give me more orange juice, will you, Tina?"

She held a glass of orange juice up to his face and placed the flexible straw in his mouth.

"Hang-gliding sure looks pretty," Fletch said. He was sitting on the picnic table, his bare feet on the bench.

"It's a pretty thing to do," Tom said. "It feels pretty. It is pretty. Soar like a bird."

"Birds get broken backs very often?" Fletch asked.

"Sometimes you land pretty hard," Tina said. "This was to be Tom's last flight before we get married next Saturday."

"Yeah," Tom said. "I was going to give it up because Tina wanted me to. She said I might get hurt. Shows you what she knows." Tom grinned at her.

"Wedding put off?" Fletch asked.

"No," Tom said. "Instead of wearing a tuxedo Tina's going to put a big red bow ribbon on my ass."

"That'll be nice," Fletch said. "At least she'll know what she's marrying. How long you going to be wrapped up like that, in plaster and aluminum?"

"Weeks," Tom groaned. "Months."

"We'll be married a long time," Tina said quietly. "A few months won't matter."

She had offered Fletch breakfast, and he was hungry, but he had refused. He figured she had enough to do taking care of Tom.

"You heard what I did?" Fletch asked.

"Yeah," Tom said. "Jack Carradine called me. At first I thought he was telling me a funny story. Then I realized he doesn't think it's even slightly funny. Somebody ran your piece on Wagnall-Phipps on his pages while he was out of town. You quoted a dead man, Fletch."

"And got fired."

"And got fired. Makes me look all the better." Tom smiled at Fletch. "Which, under the circumstances, I don't mind at all. The only job security

I've got. You screwed up royally on a story originally assigned to me."

"Tom, can you tell me any reason why Charles Blaine should show me, and let me quote from, recent memos he said were from Thomas Bradley?"

"Sure," Tom said. "He's a creep. They're all creeps at Wagnall-Phipps. Tom Bradley was a creep."

"In what way?"

"I don't know. Bradley lived way back, down deep inside himself—somewhere near his lower spine. He never seemed very real to me, if you know what I mean. Every word, gesture seemed calculated. Very self-protective. Always gave you the feeling he was hiding something—which is why we started that investigation into the financial dealings of Wagnall-Phipps a couple of years ago. Creepy. Made us suspicious. Sure enough, there he was, doing kick-backs, pay-offs, running the ski house in Aspen neither he nor any of the other executives, employees of Wagnall-Phipps ever used. He was his own worst enemy."

"Want some coffee, Tom?" Tina asked.

"Luke-warm decaffinated coffee through a glass straw," Tom said. "No, thanks."

"You, Fletch?"

"No thank you kindly, Tina."

"Then I'll go wash up the breakfast dishes." She carried the dirty plates and cups into the house.

Fletch asked, "Bradley never used the Aspen ski house himself?"

"Naw. Wasn't much of an athlete."

"How do you know?"

"We checked pretty thoroughly on who was

using that ski house and who wasn't. Just politicians and purchasing agents. Bradley never went there. He never took his kids there. Sometimes his sales manager would go and play host for a drinking weekend. If you ski and have a ski house available, you use it, right?"

"I guess so."

"Bradley's thing was making mosaics, you know? Putting together mosaics with tiny bits of colored tile. Sort of pretty. He had some he had made in his office."

"How did he get to be chairman of something called Wagnall-Phipps? Family?"

"Naw. Wagnall-Phipps was a defunct supply company. Probably they'd played the game honestly and gone broke. Bradley bought it for its debts. Doubt he put very much cash into it. Then he sold off the stock from the warehouses. I'm sure he put the price of everything up, but he made sure whoever bought from him got a kick-back, something with which to line his own pocket. So he had much more cash than he had put into the company, bought more supplies, more warehouses—he was off and running."

"When was this?"

"Oh—twenty years ago I'd guess. Then, over the years, when one of the companies that supplied him got into financial difficulty, he'd buy all of it, or part of it. So now Wagnall-Phipps is a holding company owning lots of unrelated little companies manufacturing things like rubbish barrels and sidewalk brooms and nails—stuff like that. Nobody ever said he wasn't smart. And, of course, it's still a general supply company. You should know all this, Fletch. You did a story on the company last week. Remember?"

"Will I ever forget?"

"Blaine is sort of a turkey. I've talked with him. Always seems sort of confused, lost. Treasurer of the company. You know, one of those guys who wants to do his job nine-to-five and go home. Corcoran's all right. At least he looks you in the eye and talks straight at you."

"Alexander Corcoran, president."

"Good for you, Fletch. Did you talk to him?"

"No. Blaine said he was at a golf tournament somewhere."

"So Blaine was the only person you talked to?"

" 'Fraid so."

"Gee, Fletch. You never do any story with only one source."

"Tell me."

"Sorry, Fletch. You don't need me hitting you over the head, too. Some time I'll tell you about some of the mistakes I've made."

"As far as I knew I was doing a financial up-date on a little company the *News-Tribune* had already raked over the coals. Why should I talk to anyone other than the Vice-president and treasurer? I knew all the facts and figures he'd give me had to be on file somewhere—State Bureau of Corporations, or something. I felt safe. Why would he lie to me?"

"White people lie," Tom Jeffries said. "Black people do, too."

"Jeez, I don't understand this. Tom, had anyone ever told you Thomas Bradley was dead?"

"I don't know. I don't remember. I think if anyone had ever mentioned it to me I would have considered it with complete indifference. I mean, the company employs two, three thousand people at most. It's not a publicly held company. Wagnall-Phipps is so-what's-ville. The only reason we did that exposé on it a couple of years ago—whenever we did it—was to show that it's not just the giant corporations that spread the loot around illegally."

"So if Wagnall-Phipps isn't a public company, who owns it?"

"I think it's entirely owned by Bradley. Bradley and his wife. Corcoran might have held some of the stock, but I doubt it. Wagnall-Phipps wasn't that sort of a company, you know? I never had much of a sense of family, we're-all-in-this-together kind of feeling you get from some small companies. Bradley was too laid back for that. Too much his own man. And Corcoran—call him president if you like—he was really sales manager. He didn't run the company at all. Bradley did—as chairman. I think he gave Corcoran the title of president so he'd be more effective as sales manager."

"What about the rest of Bradley's life?"

"What do you mean?"

"I mean, how could he die and nobody notice?"

"Lots of people do."

"Wasn't he important to anybody?"

"His wife. His kids. His company. Why should anyone else care?"

"Charities. Clubs. I mean, you go hang-gliding, Tom."

"Used to go."

"Used to. Didn't Bradley play golf? Tennis? You said he wasn't athletic."

"Well, I don't know, but he looked soft to me.

Not like anyone who jogged, or anything. Maybe he wasn't well."

"Politics. Didn't he have any life other than the company?"

"I didn't know him that well. I'd see him in his office. Very quiet spoken. He made those mosaics I told you about. They were nice, but I don't suppose they excited too many people. I don't know what you want, Fletch."

"I'm trying to get a handle on this guy."

"Try the cemetery."

"Very funny. I want to know why Blaine referred to him as alive when he's dead."

"Ask Blaine."

"I'm going to."

"Listen, Fletch, screwing the press isn't exactly a new game. Purposely feeding us false information so they can deny it later and make us look bad? People do it all the time. You know that."

"Talking about a dead man as being alive?"

"It's a wierd one," Tom said.

"There were kids involved. Bradley's kids. People say to them 'I saw your Daddy's name in the newspapers the other day. What a fine man he must be!' Shit, Tom, that's cruel."

"That's sick."

"Sick and cruel. So why would anyone do it?"

"Go ask the guy who did it."

"Yeah." Fletch jumped off the table. "Have a happy wedding."

"I will," Tom said. "I told Tina she'll always be able to say I took this marriage lying down."

"Anything you need before I go?"

"Yeah. Tell Tina I need her black hands out here spongin' me off. I'm gettin' sweaty."

10

James St. E. Crandall was seventy and stooped.

He stood on the porch of his shabby house in Newtowne, hands in the pockets of his dark green, baggy work pants. His eyes had not left Fletch's face since Fletch had driven onto the dirt driveway.

"Morning." Fletch smiled as he approached the steps to the porch.

"Don't want any," Crandall said.

"Any what?"

"Any whatever you got."

"You don't know what I've got."

"Don't care to know."

"You sure?"

"Absolute sure. You might just as well back that tin can you're drivin' back out into traffic and be on your way."

"Are you James St. E. Crandall?"

"None of your business."

"Are you James St. E. Crandall or not?"

"Want me to call the cops?"

"Sure," Fletch said. "I'll wait."

The weathered skin around Crandall's eyes puckered. "What makes you think you have a right to know anything?"

"I have a right to know everything."

"Who says?"

Fletch grinned. "Why do you ask?"

"You're a young punk."

"That may be."

"Don't even wear shoes. Standin' there in the dirt like white trash. Where'd you come from? You go to church? Where'd you get my name?"

"So you are James St. E. Crandall."

"Maybe."

"If you are, then I found your wallet."

"Didn't lose my wallet."

"Your passport wallet."

"Never had a passport. Never had a passport wallet."

"Have you stayed at The Park Worth Hotel lately?"

"Haven't stayed anywhere but at home."

Fletch ran his eyes over the bungalow. The paint was so thin the wood was dried out. On the porch was one rocking chair. A burst cushion was in its seat.

"I guess you never stayed at The Park Worth Hotel."

"Never heard of it."

"Do you have a son, a grandson named James St. E. Crandall?"

"None of your business."

"Look, mister. I found this wallet, see? It has money in it. And the name James St. E. Crandall. I'm trying to give the wallet back to its owner."

"It's not mine. I said that."

"Your son's?"

"Never had any children. My damned wife died thirty years ago, God rot her soul. Never had any nephews I ever heard of, and if I did, I hope they're perishin' in jail."

"You're a nice guy. You go to church?"

" 'Course I do."

"You ever heard of anyone else in the world named James St. E. Crandall?"

"Wouldn't care if I had."

"Sorry to have bothered you," Fletch said. "Nice passin' the time of day with you."

"Let me see your license and registration."

Fletch was still within the limits of Newtowne when the police car came up behind him, growled its siren at him, and pulled him over.

He handed the officer his papers.

"Irwin Maurice Fletcher," the policeman read. "What kind of a name is that?"

"A stinky name. My parents were expecting a skunk."

"Did they get one?"

"No, they had a nice kid."

"And what kind of a scam is their nice kid pullin' now?"

"I don't get you," Fletch said.

The policeman continued to hold Fletch's papers in his hand. "Well, you go up to a man's door and tell him you found his wallet and there's money in it. What's the swindle?"

"Jeez. Crandall did call the cops."

"Never mind who called."

"What a grouchy guy."

"You want to come down to the police station and explain yourself?"

"I'll explain myself here, officer."

"I'm listenin'."

"I found a wallet with the name James St. E. Crandall in it. No address. I'm trying to find the James St. E. Crandall it belongs to. I asked the one you've got here in your town and he damned near threw me off his place. And called you."

"Let me see the wallet."

"Why?"

"To save yourself from being arrested for trying a confidence game."

"You haven't enough proof for that."

"To save yourself from being arrested for driving with no shoes on."

"You can only give me a ticket for that."

Referring to Fletch's license, the policeman wrote out a ticket. "Twenty-five dollars fine," the policeman said.

"Don't retire until you get my check."

The policeman handed Fletch the ticket. "Let me see the wallet."

"No."

"Are you leaving town?"

"Trying to."

The policeman handed Fletch his license and registration. "Just keep on drivin', Irwin."

"Yes, sir."

"By the way," the policeman said, "your parents did have a skunk for a kid. What would you call someone tryin' to swindle senior citizens?"

"I wouldn't call him," Fletch said. "I'd wait for him to call me."

11

The odor of cooked hamburger wafted through the screen door. All that morning Fletch had only had coffee.

"Hi, good lookin'," the woman said to him through the Blaine's screen door. Through the door she looked down at Fletch's bare feet and smiled and ran her eyes up his body again. "What can I do you for?"

She was a bosomy woman in her mid-sixties, wearing a yellow turtleneck sweater, tight slacks and sneakers.

"How's Mister Blaine today?" Fletch asked.

"How would I know?" The woman's brown eyes were lively.

"Isn't this Charles Blaine's house?"

"Yes."

"Doesn't he have the flu?"

"Hope not. It would ruin his vacation."

"He's on vacation?"

"San Orlando. 'Way down on the Mexican coast. They've been in Mexico before, 'bout two years ago."

"Sorry," Fletch said. "I'm not explaining myself. I'm just surprised. I was told he had the flu. My name is Fletcher. *News-Tribune.* Mister Blaine helped me with a story last week on Wagnall-Phipps. There were some things wrong with the story. Thought I'd better come back and talk with Mister Blaine again."

"Fletcher, Fletcher, Fletcher," the woman said. "You the one wrote that story on what rip-off artists some funeral directors are?"

"No."

"Thought I knew your name. You hungry?"

"Of course."

"That's the right answer. All good men are hungry all the time." She held the screen door open for him. "I'll make you a hamburger."

"Wow."

"You're going to say that's right nice of me."

"Yeah."

"No need. It gives this woman a great deal of pleasure to feed a hungry man." The screen door swung closed behind Fletch. "My name's Happy Franscatti," she said.

"You are happy. I mean, you are a happy person."

"Yes, I am." She led the way through the livingroom and diningroom into the kitchen. "I've lost a husband and two children in three separate accidents."

"That's God-awful."

"Yes, it is. But I'm still a happy person. I was just born cheerful, I guess." She slapped three hamburger patties onto the grill. "I suspect it has something to do with the body chemistry. It's in the glands, or something. I know people who have no particular problems, but they act terrible sad all the time." She spoke loudly over the sizzle of the hamburgers. "They just have no capacity for happiness. I wake up every morning five-thirty, and the day's song is already goin' in my heart. I run to the window and peek out at the world to see what the day will bring. Why aren't you sitting down?"

Fletch sat at the small kitchen table.

"I'm Mary Blaine's aunt," Happy said. "You met Mary? Mrs. Blaine?"

"No. I've only met with him. In his office."

"I'm just house sitting." She turned over the hamburger, saying: "This is how you keep the juice in. Turn 'em over quick. They called me Thursday noon and said they had a chance to get away to Mexico and could I come right away? I was happy to. You should see my apartment. No, you shouldn't see my apartment. It's so small if I gain ten pounds I won't even be able to visit myself."

"They didn't know they were going ahead of time?"

"I guess not. Had supper with them Saturday night, and they didn't mention it. Not at all like Charley. He doesn't even go to the grocery store without preparing an hour and a half ahead of time, making a list, checking it twice, counting his money, changing his clothes twice. Until you're ready to yell at him. I came over Thursday noon, drove them to the airport. They were on the three-thirty flight."

"Okay," Fletch said. "His secretary told me Thursday he had the flu."

"Maybe he did. He looked pale and didn't have that much to say, although Charley never does."

"How long are they gone for?"

"Two weeks. Maybe three. Said they'd let me know. Something was wrong with the story you wrote for the newspaper?"

"My fault. I didn't check something I thought was obvious."

"You in trouble for it?"

"No," said Fletch. "I was fired."

Happy put the three hamburger patties on three buns, pressed their tops down on them, and piled them all in one plate. "If someone gave you a bum steer," she said, "it wasn't Charley. He's not capable of it. I've known him twenty years. He's too literal-minded to lie." She put the plate in front of Fletch. "He's a pest, the way he has to know the literal truth about everything: how much did this cost, how much did that cost, what store did this come from, whom exactly did you see and what exactly did they say. Drives Mary and me nuts. Truth is, we can't remember all those little things. What store did we buy something in? Who cares except Charley?"

Looking at the hamburgers, Fletch said, "Are all these for me?"

"Can't you eat them?"

"Of course."

"I've eaten. Want milk?"

"Yes. Please."

Happy brought a glass to the refrigerator and filled it with milk. "Mary's more like me. More happy-go-lucky. Of course next to Charley the Statue of Liberty looks like a stand-up comedian."

"These are good," Fletch said munching. "Has Charley worked twenty years with Wagnall-Phipps?"

"No. Just the last four. Before that he was with I.B.M." Happy brought the glass of milk to the table and sat down across from Fletch. "You don't know Charley very well."

"I don't know him at all," Fletch said.

"He's one of those people, you know, you make a joke and instead of laughing he analyses it. And then he explains it back to you—the person who made the joke in the first place. I like Charley. He makes me wonder. I think he has the body chemistry of a mica schist."

"What a mike-a-shits?"

"A kind of rock. I should have said basalt. Enough ketchup?"

"Thanks. Do you know the Bradleys, Happy?"

"Charley's boss? Yeah. Met them two or three times when Charley first went to work at Wagnall-Phipps. Haven't seen them in two or three years. I don't think they socialize much. I suspect that after Mary and Charley and Tom and Enid had dinners back and forth when Charley first went to work for Wagnall-Phipps—you know, did the necessary boss–new employee drinks and dinner things—and then everybody retreated into their own little holes. They're all a bunch of deadheads. Except Mary."

"Did you go to Tom Bradley's funeral?"

"How can you tell when a guy like that is

dead?" Happy laughed. "I don't mean to be unkind. No, I buried my younger daughter only a year and a half ago. I knew Tom Bradley had been sick—in and out of hospital—had gone east to the specialists. He was so sick his wife, Enid Bradley, was running the company. Wouldn't think her capable of it, even with the help of Charley and Alex. That's Alex Corcoran, president of Wagnall-Phipps. Alex has got some life. You know—what's your name—Fletch?—when you go through three deaths of your own, as I did, people aren't apt to rush at you with news of every other death. Invite you to every funeral, you know?"

Fletch bit into his third hamburger. "Good."

Her eyes were smiling at him. "It's very nice watching a man eat."

"Wish you'd popularize that notion."

"Not married yet, Fletch?"

"Divorced."

"At your age? What happened? Couldn't your wife figure out how to work your diaper pin?"

"Something like that."

"She didn't feed you. Girls today. It's against their pride to feed a man. It's also against their pride a man should pick up a restaurant check. So everybody's starving."

"Tell me about Enid and Tom Bradley, Happy."

"What do you mean?"

"You said he was sick. Sick with what?"

"I forget. One of those long-range things. What would that be?"

"I don't know."

"Not a very big man. No bigger than his wife. He used to tell dirty jokes I liked. There was something especially dirty about them when he told them. I don't know. I suppose it was because he was the boss. And I always felt the dirty jokes sort of embarrassed Enid. She'd laugh, but only as if she had to."

"Maybe she'd heard them before."

"I suppose so. I really didn't know them very well." Happy looked at the wall clock. "I've got to get going."

"Oh. Okay." Fletch drained his glass of milk. "Anything I can do for you, Happy? Can I give you a lift anywhere?"

"No, thanks." She took Fletch's empty plate and glass to the sink. "I'll just get my guitar and be on my way."

"Guitar?"

"Yeah, I always bring it when I go to the Senior Citizens' Home. I play for them, and we sing. Some of them sing quite well. An old person's singing voice can be very fine. Too bad the world doesn't notice."

She went into a bedroom. Fletch waited in the front hall.

"Here we are," Happy said. She came through the bedroom carrying a guitar case and five or six copies of *The National Review*. Fletch opened the screen door for her. "Just slam the door behind you."

"Happy, thank you very much for lunch."

"My pleasure."

"Have a nice time at the Senior Citizens' Home this afternoon."

"Sure," Happy said. "I've got to go burden the old folks with my cheer. I've got too much of it to keep all to myself."

77

12

Fletch drove by the Bradley house in Southworth, saw the Cadillac in the driveway, saw a man in the driveway two houses down painting a thirty foot sailboat on a trailer hitch, continued through the executive-homes neighborhood until he came back to the main road, turned left, stopped at a gas station, took slacks, a jacket, shirt, loafers and socks from the trunk of his M.G., went into the rest room and changed.

Then he drove back to the street the Bradley house was on and parked three houses beyond it.

He walked back to the driveway where the man was painting the boat. He went up the driveway and stood next to the man, who was dressed in shorts and a paint-spotted sweat shirt. "Hi," Fletch said. "That's a wood boat."

The man smiled at him. "She sure is." The man was in his late thirties and still had freckles across his nose. "She's my wood boat and she'll never be your wood boat. Not for sale."

He had put green garbage bags on the driveway to catch the paint. Not much had spilled.

"I'm in real estate," Fletch said. "The question I have to ask you is one I really hate to ask."

"My house isn't for sale, either."

"Not your's," Fletch said. "The Bradley's."

"Oh, them." The man glanced in the direction of the Bradley's house.

"When we hear of a death of the head of a household, we have to ask if anybody thinks that house might go on the market. At least my boss says I have to."

"What firm you work with?"

"South Southworth Realty." Fletch said it in such a way the man might think he was stuttering.

"You work for Paul Krantz?"

"Yeah."

"I know Paul. He helped put together a real estate deal for my father a few years ago."

"Nice man, Paul is," Fletch said.

"So you'd rather ask a neighbor about a widow's intentions than ask the widow herself."

"Wouldn't you?"

"Yes. Except the neighbor might not know."

"Your guess would be better than mine."

The man was applying the creamy white paint thickly to the wood. "Is Tom Bradley dead?" the man asked.

"So we hear."

"I thought so, too. In fact I could say I knew so. Then I read an article in the newspaper the other day, the *News-Tribune*, that made him seem very much alive. Couldn't believe my eyes. I read the piece twice and then showed it to my wife. I had to ask her if I'd gone crazy."

"Yeah." Fletch stood on one foot and then the other.

"Did you read it?"

"I never read the financial pages," Fletch said. "Perhaps I should."

"Not that the financial pages of the *News-Tribune* are that good. Their sports pages are better."

Fletch looked up at the clean, curtained windows of the house. "Is Tom Bradley dead or not?"

"Enid Bradley said so."

"When?"

"At a Christmas party we gave. Every year we give one, just for people in the neighborhood. Every year we invite the Bradleys—just because they live here. They never came. This year, Enid came. At some point during the party, my wife came to me and said, 'Did you know Tom Bradley is dead? Enid just mentioned it.' I went and spoke to Enid. First we'd heard of it. This neighborhood isn't that close, but, gee, when a guy dies two houses away from you, you expect to hear about it."

"Enid Bradley told you Thomas Bradley is dead?"

The man squinted through the sunlight at Fletch. "Enid Bradley told me Thomas Bradley is dead," he said exactly. "She told me last Christmas. Then I see his name in the newspaper the other day. Do you understand it?"

"Ah," Fletch said. "I guess newspapers have been known to be wrong."

"Come on. Quoting a dead man?"

"I suppose it can happen," Fletch said.

"Will you tell me how?"

"I wish I could. If Mrs. Bradley says her husband is dead..."

"...then he must be dead. Right?"

"They have a couple of kids, haven't they?"

"Yeah."

Fletch waited for more, but none came. He gathered the neighborhood did not have much positive enthusiasm for the Bradley young. The man spent longer than usual putting paint on his brush.

"Nice boat," Fletch finally said. "You take good care of it."

"I guess I can say to you," the man said, "seeing you work for Paul Krantz—and I consider him a friend—that the Bradleys are not the most popular neighbors."

"I see."

"I'd be polite to say they're loud."

"Loud?"

"They've had their problems, I guess. Loud—you know what I mean—screams in the night, shouting, doors slamming, the kids burning rubber as they drive away from the house two, three o'clock in the morning. The occasional smashed window."

Fletch looked around. All the houses were set well back from the road, and from each other. "You hear things like that here?"

"You wouldn't think so. And talking to Enid Bradley, looking at her, you'd think she was the quietest, most demure little lady you ever met. But sometimes at night we'd hear her screaming like a stuck pig. Hysterical shouting and screaming. We never heard his voice at all." Again the man stirred the paint thoughtfully with his brush before lifting it. "Tom Bradley tried suicide two or three years ago."

"You know that?"

"The rescue squad came early Sunday morning. We saw them bring the stomach pump into the house, and then carry him off strapped to a stretcher. The whole neighborhood saw it. And he didn't take too many pills by accident. It was after one of those all-night shouts, you know?"

"Maybe he was sick," Fletch said. "Maybe he had been told he was fatally ill, or something, you know? I mean, he did die."

"I don't know, either. But I do know the screaming and shouting went on in that house for as long as we've lived here. Five or six years. Deep emotional problems. That family had deep emotional problems. I suspect there's a family like that in every neighborhood, from the slums to a neighborhood like this, for the lower-rich. Feel sorry for them, but what the hell can we do?"

"Has all that stopped? I mean, the noise and the smashed windows, since Tom Bradley died?"

"Yeah. It's become a very quiet house. The kids come and go, but there are no more slamming doors and burning rubber. Of course, she—I mean Enid—goes off to work nearly every day now. Or so my wife tells me. I think someone told me she's trying to run her husband's company—I forget the name of it, oh, yeah, Wagnall-Phipps is what the *News-Tribune* said—until she can get someone else to take over. Of course if the *News-Tribune* said Wagnall-Phipps, the company might be called anything including Smith, Smith and Smith."

"Yeah," Fletch said. *"News-Tribune.* Yuck. Punk paper."

"They have a good sports section."

"Mrs. Bradley didn't say anything to you about selling the house?"

"Haven't seen her since Christmas. Months ago. Live two houses away and I don't think anyone in the neighborhood actually converses with anyone in that house, year after year. We've heard enough of their noise. We're all embarrassed, I guess. You understand."

"Sure."

"I wish you would go ask Mrs. Bradley if she's moving. It might give her the idea that she should."

"Yeah."

"This is a nice neighborhood. It would be great to have a nice family in that house. You know, a family that didn't embarrass us all when we look at them?" The man moved his paint bucket nearer the stern of the boat. "Tell her her house is worth a lot of money, and you can find her a nice condominium down nearer the center of town—one with padded walls."

13

"Would you like a drink, Mister Fletcher?"
Enid Bradley asked.

"No. Thank you."

"I think I will."

Fletch was sitting in the broad, deep divan of
Enid Bradley's livingroom. Through sliding glass
doors sparkled a good-sized swimming pool.

Enid Bradley moved across the livingroom to
a bar disguised as a book case and poured herself
a large glass of white wine. "Seeing I must go to
the office every day during this period, relaxing
with a drink Saturday afternoon is quite all right,
isn't it? Isn't that the excuse you men always use
for drinking on the weekend?"

"No."

"You are younger than I was expecting, Mister Fletcher."

Enid Bradley did not seem relaxed to Fletch.

She seemed someone eager to show she was re-laxed. Her eyes had been too searching in his face when she opened the door to him; her sigh had been too deep when he identified himself. She was an over-weight woman in her mid-forties in a slightly out-of-date dress and high-heeled shoes. Fletch could not guess what she might have been doing before the doorbell rang. The only image that came to his mind was that of her standing somewhere in the house, fearfully anticipating him, or some other threatening visitor.

She sat in a chair placed at a slight angle to the coffee table, and to him. The surface of the coffee table was bright inlaid tile.

Fletch put his fingertips on the mosaic. "Did your husband make this?"

"Yes."

"It's very nice."

"There are several around the house. In the den. In our bedroom. In a table by the pool." Her eyelids hooded as she turned her face toward the light from the glass doors. Then her free hand gestured over her shoulder. "And, of course, there's that one, on the wall."

There was a large mosaic of precisely shaded concentric circles, brightest at the center, on the wall next to the fireplace.

"I don't blame you for coming to see me, Mister Fletcher. If I'm offended, I'm also curious." She put her glass on the coffee table. "I read your article about our company in Wednesday's *News-Tribune*. I was obliged to call your managing editor. It was just too upsetting to my children and, of course, the employees."

"I regret that."

"Where did you ever get the idea of quoting my husband?"

Saying nothing, Fletch just looked at her.

"We're not suing the newspaper. What's the use? I didn't even ask your managing editor, that Mister Jaffe, to print a retraction. I can't imagine what it would say. 'The recent article on Wagnall-Phipps Incorporated by I.M. Fletcher erroneously had quotes by the late Thomas Bradley'? No, that would just stir up more confusion. More hurt."

"You might let the *News-Tribune* print an obituary on your husband. They never have."

"Rather late now, isn't it?"

"When exactly did your husband die, Mrs. Bradley?"

"A year ago this month."

Fletch sighed. "A year ago this month. I saw memos from him dated as recently as three weeks ago."

"You couldn't have. I mean, how could you have? Why do you say you did? The idea is absurd. You see, Mister Fletcher, I have the choice of thinking you're a very sick young man. You've done a very cruel thing to me and my family."

"Or—?"

"What do you mean, 'Or—?' "

"You said you had a choice. Either I'm very sick, or, what?"

"Or someone else is. The reason I'm talking to you, didn't close the door in your face, is because I have a suspicion. At first I thought your article was just another effort on the part of your newspaper to smear Wagnall-Phipps—as you did a few years ago. But, no, what you did was too, too absurd. It doesn't leave your newspaper a leg to stand on. I was even going to ask your Mister Jaffee if I could see you, talk to you, but—well, he discouraged me."

"How did he do that?"

"He said you're very young, which you are, and that young people make mistakes, which they do."

"You settled on the conclusion that I'm very sick."

"Yes and no. I did and I didn't." She brought her glass of wine to her lips and replaced it on the coffee table. No wine seemed missing from the glass. "I've taken another step..." She hesitated. "...which is more to my purpose, if you know what I mean."

"No. I don't."

Enid Bradley shrugged. "It really can't be important to me, Mister Fletcher, if you are a sick, cruel man—as long as you don't hurt me or my family again." In her lap, her fingernails worried each other. "It's very hard for me. You must understand. Wagnall-Phipps was Thomas' company. He built it and he ran it. For the last twenty years I've been a housewife and mother. But at least for now I'm trying to run the company."

Sympathetic phrases plodded through Fletch's mind but he gave voice to none of them.

"But your editor, Mister Carraway, came out Thursday night."

"Carradine."

"Is his name Carradine? I was so upset. He sat with me and my children, Tom and Ta-ta. He was very kind. He was more explicit."

"About what?"

Her eyes flashed into his. "He said you're a fool, Mister Fletcher. That you're always doing wild and stupid things. He said you're an office joke. He said you're a compulsive liar." Her eyes fell. "He also said you were to be fired the next day, and that you'd never work in the newspaper business again."

"Say, he was kind."

Her eyes looked into his again, with less anger. "Were you fired?"

"Of course."

"Then, from your own point of view, why are you pursuing this matter further?"

"Because I'm a good journalist and I've got two statements, or impressions, which don't match."

"Are you sure you're not just being cruel?"

"Mrs. Bradley, I wrote a newspaper article quoting your husband. I never heard of your husband before, or you, or your family, and if I'd ever heard of Wagnall-Phipps it meant nothing to me. Then I'm told your husband is dead. I'm shocked. I'm hurt by this, too."

Her voice squeaked drily. "Do you think I'm lying to you?"

"The *News-Tribune* did not print an obituary on your husband. I haven't been able to check the Bureau of Vital Statistics yet, because it's Saturday and I just got back to town last night. But I will on Monday."

"It will do you no good," said Enid Bradley. "At least, I don't think so. My husband died in Switzerland."

"Oh."

"I thought everyone knew that. He was cremated there."

"I see."

Expressing exasperation, she rose from her chair, crossed the room, took a hand-sized, decorated box from the mantel and placed it on the coffee table in front of Fletch. "These are his ashes, Mister Fletcher."

Fletch stared at the filigreed box lid.

"Open it," she said. "Go ahead. Open it."

"I don't need to."

She opened it. Inside were ashes, looking as if they had settled toward the center while still wet.

"Do you have any more questions, Mister Fletcher?"

"Yes," he said. He cleared his throat. "Yes."

She sat in the chair again. "I will tell you everything," she said, "if you will just go away and stop this insane harrassing of us."

"Yes," he said. "Of course."

"My husband had a form of blood cancer. Which means that, in order to stay alive, his blood had to be changed regularly. That is, his own blood had to be drawn out while fresh blood was being pumped into him. You can imagine what a horror that is."

"Yes. I'm sorry," he said. He closed the lid of the box.

"You're going to hear me out."

"Yes. Of course."

"You can imagine how debilitating all that is—having your own blood drained out while new blood is being pumped in. No, of course you can't."

"Yes," Fletch said. "No."

"Over time, of course, it weakened him more and more. Poor Thomas. Running the company he wanted no one to know how sick he was. Alex Corcoran, the president, is really only chief of sales—a big, hale-and-hearty fellow whose mind is permanently stuck on golf. In fact, he's playing in some tournament over at the Southworth Country Club this afternoon. Charley Blaine, the Vice-president and treasurer, is a superb backroom man, but one of the most dependent characters you ever saw in your life. If everything isn't just perfect, he overreacts and does crazy things. And Thomas was the kind of man who didn't want his children worrying about him. They're beautiful, happy, successful children. Ta-ta—our daughter, Roberta—is teaching at her old prep school, Southworth Preparatory, and half-way through her first teaching year they've made her, Head of House. And Tom is finishing up his premedical studies at the College. They are both doing extremely well. My husband wanted to live. But these treatments, these blood exchanges, had to happen more and more frequently. It was a cumulative disease, Mister Fletcher. He was getting weaker and weaker.

"Then we heard about this new technique the doctors in Switzerland had developed. I can't pretend to understand it, or explain it. It has something to do with not letting the new blood mingle with the old blood, during the exchange. I take it you don't know anything about medicine, either?"

"No."

"Vacuums or something were to be created in the body. I'm not sure only Swiss doctors are doing it, but Thomas heard about this doctor in Switzerland who was the first, or the best, or something. The most respected. So, while I stayed to run the company as well as I could, he went to

Switzerland for these extensive treatments. All the news was good. He was doing fine. And then he died."

She was looking directly at Fletch as she spoke, rather in the manner of someone insulted. Then she put a hand to her brow and squeezed her eyes shut.

"Mister Fletcher, will you please leave us alone, and stop this insanity of yours?"

Fletch tried to make himself comfortable in the soft divan. He took a deep breath and exhaled slowly. "Mrs. Bradley," he said, "why did your Vice-president and treasurer, Charles Blaine, refer last week to your husband as alive? Why did he show me recently dated memos purportedly from your husband?"

Enid Bradley raised her head and blinked her eyes around the upper corners of the room. She spoke gently. "That's why I'm seeing you, Mister Fletcher. I'm now convinced of your innocence— that you meant to do nothing cruel. I'm afraid we're both victims of someone else's sickness."

"Why would he do such a thing, Mrs. Bradley?"

"Charley is a worrisomely tight man, if you know what I mean. Anything out of the ordinary rattles him. He was terribly fond—worshipful—of my husband. Thomas would make the silliest little joke, and Charley would repeat it and laugh all night. I tried to break the news of Thomas' death gently. No, I did not offer the local newspapers obituaries. No, I did not run a memorial service for him locally. Maybe I should have. Maybe if I had done so all this painful confusion would have been avoided. You see, I took over the company only in Thomas' absence. Everybody believed he was coming back. Then Thomas died. I didn't know what to do. Thank God for Francine. She's been such a help." Enid Bradley looked into her lap. "She suggested I break the news slowly, gently, to each person individually—which I did. I even waited months—until last fall—to tell people, so the hurt of his death would be somewhat removed from them. I don't think Charley ever accepted Thomas' death. I think it drove Charley off the deep end. He didn't see Thomas die, so he doesn't believe Thomas died."

"Who is Francine?"

"Thomas' sister. She lives in New York. She and Thomas were always extremely close."

"Mrs. Bradley, how do you explain the memos I saw from your husband?"

"If you saw such memos, Mister Fletcher, then they were forgeries. Obviously. Charles Blaine forged them. What else am I to think? Once or twice, Charley has referred to Thomas as alive, in speaking to me. You know, referred to Thomas in the present tense. I thought his tongue was just slipping. Then, when I saw your article . . . Wednesday night . . . I figured it out. Charley must be having some sort of a nervous breakdown. Thursday morning I told Charley, as forcefully as I could, that Thomas is dead and has been dead for a year. Then I sent him and his wife away for a long vacation."

"Mexico."

"Is that where they went? Oh, yes, I think they've gone to Mexico before for their vacations. We'll just have to see how he is when he comes back. If he really went so far as forgery . . . I don't know. You don't have any copies of those memos, do you, Mister Fletcher?"

"No."

"Well. You see. I haven't known what to do. It's all been very difficult."

"Do you intend to continue running the company, Mrs. Bradley?"

"No! Thank God." She appeared horrified at the thought.

"Are you selling out?"

"No. That wouldn't be fair to the children. No, Francine is coming West to take over the company, as soon as she can settle up her own business in New York. She's much cleverer than I. As I said, she and Thomas were very much alike. It's almost as if they had the same mind. She's run businesses before." Enid Bradley looked absently across the room. "She should be able to come West in a couple of months."

Fletch said, "I guess I don't know what to say."

Enid said, "There is nothing to say. I'm sure you didn't mean any harm. It's just that the man you were talking to was temporarily deranged. How could you have known that? If you like, I'll call your managing editor again. Tell him that you and I talked. Tell him about Charley, and how insanely fond he was of my husband...."

"Thank you, but it wouldn't do any good. I'm famous in the business now for having quoted someone who wasn't alive at the time. I'll never live that down."

"Mister Fletcher, is there anything I can do to help you? Reporters don't make much money, I know, and now you've lost your job. I guess it's partly our fault. I should have known Charley Blaine was going off the deep end."

"That's very nice of you, but no, thanks. It

was nice of you to see me, under the circumstances."

"This is all very distressing."

Enid Bradley rose and showed Fletch to the door. Neither said another word.

14

"Cold beer," Fletch said. "If you've got any left."

The barman at the Nineteenth Hole, the bar of the Southworth Country Club, looked Fletch in the face, obviously considered challenging him, then drew a beer and put it in front of Fletch.

"Thanks," Fletch smiled. During a tournament weekend there were apt to be many strangers in and out of a golf club.

At the end of the bar near the windows overlooking the greens was a large and noisy group of men dressed casually. Two couples in the room, at tables, were dressed for dinner.

"Pebble Beach," said one of the noisy men. "Nobody believes what I did at Pebble Beach. Even I don't believe what I did at Pebble Beach!"

And they said this and they said that and they

laughed at almost everything. Fletch sipped his beer.

His glass was nearly empty when one of the men turned to another, a heavily-built man wearing bifocals, and said, "Alex, I thought you'd never really get over your bug-a-boo about approaching the seventh green."

"Well," Alex smiled. "I did. Just in time."

Fletch picked up his beer, moved down the bar and, laughing with the men, looking interested at the next thing to be said, insinuated himself into the group. He nodded in appreciation at their slightly drunken inanities. He stood next to the man called Alex.

After many minutes, at a fairly quiet point in the conversation, Fletch said to the man, "You're Alex Corcoran, aren't you?"

"Sure," the man said.

"Second place winner of not the biggest but surely the friendliest golf tournament in the U.S. of A.," slurred one of the group.

"Congratulations," Fletch said.

"It's you young guys who beat me now," Corcoran said. "And you don't even go to bed at night to sleep." He pulled on his gin and tonic. "I said, to sleep."

"You and I met briefly before," Fletch said. "What's the name of that club over there...?" He pointed vaguely to the East.

"Euston."

"Yeah. Euston."

"Did I play you?"

"No, I wiped out in the first round. Watched you. We talked in the bar, later."

Alex Corcoran laughed. "Pardon me for not remembering."

"We talked about Wagnall-Phipps. You work for Wagnall-Phipps, right?"

"No!" said a golfer. "He doesn't work for Wagnall-Phipps. He's the president!"

"He doesn't work at all," said another.

Fletch nodded. "Yeah, I thought we talked about Wagnall-Phipps."

"Been with W-P seven years," Corcoran said. "Didn't become president, though, until the company suddenly decided to get out of the ski house business."

Everyone laughed.

"Jerry was really screwed by that." A golfer shook his head. "Jeez. Business entertaining. Suddenly it becomes illegal, or un-American or something."

"Depends on who you entertain."

"Depends on who you bribe."

Everything was funny to these golfers after the tournament.

"Alex, what happened to Jerry?"

"He's gone skiing," one of them joked.

"Yeah. Retired to Aspen."

"The ex-president of Wagnall-Phipps," said the current president, "is living in México on a pension bigger than my salary."

"Really?" marveled one of the men. "The wages of sin."

"Pretty big pension," Alex said. "The scandal did him no harm. Wish I could work up a good scandal myself. Then I'd never have to go to the office."

"You hardly ever go now, Alex."

"You can't sell our crap from behind a desk," Alex said. "You gotta get out there and dazzle by foot-work!" The big man shuffled his feet in a boxer's step. None of his drink spilled.

"Thomas Bradley," Fletch said. "Your boss. Didn't he die?"

All the men guffawed.

"Depends on which paper you read," one of them said. "Another round of drinks, Mike," he said to the bartender. "What for you?" he asked, looking into Fletch's glass. "I don't know your name."

"Mike," Fletch said. "Mike Smith."

"And a beer for Mike, Mike."

"Mike Smith? You were on the U. at Berkeley golf team, weren't you?"

"Is Thomas Bradley dead or not?" Fletch asked.

"Everywhere but in the *News-Tribune*."

Fletch looked confused.

"Yes," Alex Corcoran said in a more serious tone. "He died. About a year ago. Did you know him?"

"I knew his sister," Fletch said. "In New York. Francine."

"Oh, yeah?" Corcoran's face expressed great interest.

"Well, met her once," Fletch said. "At a party, you know?"

"What's she like?" Alex asked.

"You mean you've never met her?"

"No. She's coming out to take over the company, and I've never met her. Tom used to say she was brilliant. Never came West, as far as I know."

"How did Tom die?" Fletch asked.

"Went to France for some medical treatments and didn't survive them, is what I understand."

"France?"

"Never knew he was as sick as he was. He used to be moody, and act down-in-the-dumps once in a while. Jeez, I didn't know the guy was fatally ill—dyin'!"

"But you did know he was sick?"

"No. Not really. The only comment I made about it to my wife was that he seemed to be getting smaller. Don't ask me what I mean, because I don't know. I guess his shoulders got thinner. He must have lost weight. He wasn't very big to begin with. Poor ol' Tom. Here's to you, Tom." Alex raised his glass and tipped it like a censer before drinking.

"Nice trophy," Fletch said, nodding to it on the bar.

"Say, so you know his sister, Francine Bradley, eh?" Alex Corcoran said.

"Well, as I said, I only met her once."

"Enid says she's a real clever business woman, that this Francine and Tom used to talk all the time. Some of Tom's best ideas came from Francine, Enid said."

"I guess she's pretty clever," Fletch said.

"Tom left it in his Will that Francine was to take over operation of the company—if she was willing and able. Tell you—what's your name?"

"Mike."

"I'll tell you, Mike, I'll welcome her with open arms."

"You will? Company not running so well?"

"Well, you know, a company needs a head—

someone to make the people-decisions, give it a direction. I'm president, by the grace of Tom Bradley, but I'm not good that way. What I'm very good at is selling things to people. That's all I can do; that's all I want to do. I mean, really, my wife says I could sell snowballs to Siberians. Long-range corporate planning, the day-to-day stuff—I'm not good that way. Enid tries, but, you know..."

"Enid is Tom's wife?"

"Yeah. Nice lady. Once in a while she has a good idea, but, you know...long-range planning. Listen, anything Tom Bradley decided to do with his company is all right with me. He could have left it to his horse, and I'd say, sure, fine, good idea."

"Tom rides?"

Alex looked at him. "A figure of speech. Don't you know your Roman history?"

"Oh."

"As a matter of fact, Tom did ride. Kept a horse out in the valley, somewhere. Rode on Sundays, some week-day mornings. Yeah, he liked riding. He'd go alone, I guess."

"Sounds like you were fond of him."

"Listen." Alex's eyes became a little wet. "Fond of him...I loved that guy. He was a real gentleman. Except for his stupid, raunchy jokes everybody had always heard before. That's what was so funny about them. He was one hell of a nice man. People like that shouldn't die so young. When you consider all the shits who live a lot older—like me!"

"Gotta split." Fletch put his beer glass on the bar, and held out his hand to Alex Corcoran. "Nice talking with you. Sorry about Tom Bradley."

"Yeah, yeah. I gotta go too. My wife will be lookin' for me." Two of the other golfers in the group had left. Alex Corcoran picked his trophy up off the bar. "Come here, you little darlin'." He kissed it. "Where the hell would a man be, if it weren't for golf?"

"Home with the wife," said one of the other golfers.

And they all laughed.

15

Fletch drove home in the dark, but the lights in his apartment were on and Moxie came to the door as soon as she heard his key in the lock. She was wearing an apron and nothing else.

"Gee," Fletch said. "Just like a wife."

"Not like wife." With her fingers Moxie held the edges of the apron's skirt away from her skin and curtsied, as a geisha might. "Like Moxie Mooney."

He kissed her. "Your ex-wife called," she said. He kissed her again. "Tom Jeffries called. Wants you to call him back." He kissed her again.

"What did good ol' Linda want?"

"Oh, we talked a long time. She told me what a male nymphomaniac you are, how unreliable you are, how funny you are. She told me about the time you called her from the office and said you were on your way home and then went to Hawaii."

"There was a story in Hawaii."

"She said the meatloaf got cold. How cruel you were to her cat. I believe she loves you."

"And what did you tell her?"

"I told her I believe you still love her."

"Thanks a heap. I love paying her alimony."

"Oh, she said you haven't. Paid her any alimony, that is. I told her I didn't understand that, as you have scads of money, have just ordered a sixty-foot motor cruiser, and anytime she needs money she's to come to you, alimony be damned."

"Terrific. What else did you do for me?"

"Told her you'd just given me a diamond tiara and a mink coat."

"I'm sure she believed you."

"I don't think so, somehow. Go telephone what's-his-name. He's the guy with the broken back, isn't he?"

"Yeah."

"I'll run you a bath."

"Why don't we—?"

She put her hand against his shoulder and pushed. "Yucky, dirty, smelly boy. If I'm going to give my all for you, least you might do is remove the outer layer of pollution."

"But, but—"

"Lots of evening left."

She turned her back on him and hopped into the bathroom.

"Tom? Fletch. How's life at ground level?"

"Never, never, Fletch, have I known there were so many ants in the world. All day I spend in the patio watching ants."

From the livingroom, Fletch could hear the

bath water running. "You don't see many ants when you're hang-gliding I guess."

"Actually, ants are sort of interesting. Just like people, only more so."

"The Darwin of the patio."

"Listen, I called you not only because I'm bored out of my mind but also to tell you a funny story. Cheer you up. A story under the heading *Incompetent People Who Do Not Get Fired From The News-Tribune.*"

"There are some?"

"Jack Carradine called this morning, after you left. About Clara Snow."

"What's she done now?"

"You know she's been assigned to the State House, just as if she were a real reporter?"

"Yes."

"Well, while assigned to the State House she failed to report that the Governor's press-secretary's brother owns a car dealership which, if you can believe it, has been selling cars to the state police."

"Clara didn't report that?"

"She put her nose up in the air, looked all haughty, you know, as only she can, and said she felt the matter was too personal."

"To whom?"

"A private matter, she said. Having to do with family life. Not in the public interest to report. Then she said the state police have to buy their cars from somewhere. Can you believe that?"

"It makes me angry."

"Good. I thought it would cheer you up. Of course you know Clara's been going to bed with the press secretary."

"I thought she was going to bed with Frank Jaffe."

"Him, too. Clara goes to bed with anyone who can help her career. You can't say Clara doesn't give her all. Which is why she's being allowed to get away with this little slip of her's."

"Are you telling me Frank still isn't going to run the story?"

"Jack says Frank called the governor and told him to put an end to this corruption within a month, or the *News-Tribune* would blow the whistle. How do you like those sweet peas?"

"Jeez. I hope the competition gets wise to it."

"You could always make sure they do, Fletch."

"No. I wouldn't do that."

"Just trying to get you a job, man."

"Not that way."

"How do you feel, Fletch?"

"Lousy. How do you feel?"

"Lousy. See ya."

"See ya."

Fletch called the *News-Tribune*. There was no chance of the bathtub overflowing. Water ran into it at about the speed of decisions reached by committee.

"Classifieds," the girl said. "May I help you?"

"Yes, please," Fletch said. "I'd like to run an item in your Lost and Found column."

"Yes, sir. What's the message?"

"Wallet found name James St. E. Crandall write Box number—whatever box number you give me."

"236."

"236."

"James St. E. like in James Saint Edward or something?"

"Yes."

"C-r-a-n-d-a-l-l?"

"Yes."

"And what name and number shall I bill this to?"

"I.M. Fletcher."

"You're kidding."

"Don't think so."

"That you, Fletch?"

"Yeah."

"Hey, real sorry you got booted. What did you do, set fire to Frank Jaffe's pants?"

"I thought everyone knew."

"Yeah, I know. You quoted a stiff."

"Who is this?"

"Mary Patouch."

"Well, Mary. Want my address?"

"Fletch, I've always wanted your address. You know that."

Fletch gave her his address and then called the San Francisco Chronicle long-distance and placed the same ad.

"How did I meet Fletcher?" Moxie said like a child talking to herself. She had dropped her apron on the bathroom floor and gotten into the tub of warm water with Fletch. "I was buying a hot dog and this nice man standing next to me at the counter paid for it and then said nothing to me. So I said, 'Thank you very much, sir,' and you said,

'Seeing we're having such a terrible lunch, why don't we have dinner together?'"

"Your story is true so far. And you said, 'Yes, all right'. Why did you say, 'Yes, all right'?"

"Because you're beautiful and smooth and have funny eyes and I wanted to touch you."

"Oh. Perfectly good reason."

"Your eyes look like they're laughing all the time. Almost all the time."

"I see."

"You can't see your eyes. And at dinner I told you I had to come down here this weekend to start rehearsals Monday and you said you were driving this way next day, you had to be back at the office, ho ho ho, and why shouldn't I save bus fare by coming with you. So, seeing we were friends already, we went back to my place and..."

"...and what?"

"And touched each other."

She kissed his throat and he kissed her forehead.

"So tell me about this day," she said. "I've known you three days, but only been with you two."

"A very ordinary day," Fletch said. "Just like all the others. Met a grouchy guy who tried to throw me off his place while I was trying to do him a favor, I thought, called the cops and tried to have me arrested."

"And did the cops give you a shower and shave today?"

"Not today. A ticket for driving barefoot. Then I met a marvelous happy woman named Happy who invited me in and cooked me up three hamburgers."

"Nice of her. She wanted your bod?"

"For three hamburgers?"

"I got you for less. Jar of peanut butter."

"Charles Blaine's wife's aunt. Charles Blaine, by the way, the source of my suicidal story, has gone to Mexico."

"So you can't beat him up."

"I think I'd like to. Then I met a solid-looking man working on his boat in Southworth who looked less like a neighborhood gossip than Calvin Coolidge but who told me all the gossip about the Bradley family he could think of, and maybe then some."

"Did he know who he was talking to?"

"Of course not. Then I met the widow Bradley."

"Jeez, you're brave. Are these brass?"

"Can't take that. The gossipy neighbor said Mrs. Bradley is a midnight screamer who probably drove her husband to attempt suicide. Speaking of her, she is dignified, quiet, reasonable. She says this whole thing happened because Charles Blaine is suffering a nervous breakdown or something, which is why she sent him on vacation."

"So is Tom Bradley dead?"

"Then I went to the Southworth Country Club for a beer."

"I know."

"How do you know?"

"I can see it. Right there in your stomach." She pressed her finger against his appendix.

"Cannot."

She kissed his mouth. "I smelled it when you came in."

"Met Alex Corcoran, president of Wagnall-Phipps. Everyone says Tom Bradley's dead. The widow Bradley showed me his ashes."

"But, of course, you don't want to believe it."

"Of course I believe it. I believe everything. That's how I got into trouble in the first place."

She pushed his head below water.

"Glub."

"Face it, Fletch. You're sunk."

"Glub. Where you going?"

She was stepping out of the tub.

"Forgot the steak. Can't you smell it burning?"

"Steak! How'd you get steak?"

She had called to him, *Don't bother getting dressed—everything's ready.* She had the plates of steak and salad set out on the livingroom rug. She smiled at him when he came in.

"Opened a charge account," she said.

"Your name?"

"Of course." She poured wine into the glasses. "Can't starve forever."

"It's good. Great!"

"It's cheap and burnt," she said. "At least you'll never have to divorce me."

"Why's that? Not that I was thinking of it, already."

" 'Cause you'll never marry me."

"Oh. I was thinking of asking."

"I'll never marry anybody."

"Never ever?"

"Never ever. I'm an actor and actors should never get married."

"A lot do."

"You know about my father."

"Frederick Mooney."

" 'Nough said."

"You told me he's playing Falstaff in Toronto."

"When he's sober. Then he's playing *Salesman* in Chicago. When he's sober. Last Christmas he did a baggy-pants comic routine at a dinner theater in Florida. When he was sober."

"So he's an actor who likes to drink. Not the first. Not the last. Your dad was known as a damned fine actor. Still is, as far as I know."

"I haven't told you about my mother."

"No."

"She's in a very expensive home in Kansas for the mentally absent."

"Oh. You think that's your father's fault?"

"Packing, unpacking, packing. Putting him to bed. Getting him up. Sobering him up. Looking for him in the bars. Reminding him which God-damn play he's performing. Years of it. Taking care of me, on the road. Putting up with his women. His disappearances. His tensions. His paranoias. She couldn't take the day anymore, let alone the night. Something just snapped."

"Okay," he said. "How much of that had to do with his acting?"

"All of it."

"You sure?"

"I'm sure."

"Then why do you want to be an actor?"

"I don't want to be an actor." Instinctively she moved her head so that the light fell on her nose beautifully. "I am an actor."

He drank his wine. "Come on. Eat up."

"Also I'd like to be able to pay my mother's bills when that day comes that Freddy no longer can do."

"Thanks for the steak," Fletch said. "Eat yours up, or I'll attack you instantly."

Moxie picked up her knife and fork. "So what are you going to do tomorrow?"

Fletch shrugged. "Guess spend another day going around apologizing to people."

"Who's left?"

"The Bradley kids."

Moxie nodded. "Your piece must have been a real shock to them."

"I wouldn't feel right not touching base with them."

"You'll come to the cocktail party tomorrow night at the Colloquial Theater?"

"Sure. I'll go with you."

"Do me a favor, though, uh?"

"Anything."

"Don't mention Freddy."

"Frederick Mooney. A famous name."

"Infamous," she said. "Infamous."

16

As Fletch walked by he noticed the boat still in the driveway, gleaming white under its fresh coat of paint under the three o'clock in the morning moonlight. Except for the street lights, there was only one light visible in the neighborhood, a coach lantern several houses down.

In bare feet he went up the Bradley's driveway and into the opened garage. The door to the house was locked. He went around the house to the kitchen door, which was also locked.

The glass door between the livingroom and the pool area slid open with a rumble. Houses away, a dog barked.

The moonlight did not do much to lighten the livingroom. Fletch stood inside the door a moment, listening, letting his eyes become used to the deeper darkness.

Putting each foot forward slowly, he walked to

the fireplace. The box of ashes was not on the mantel.

He went to the coffee table and stooped over it. With loose fingers he combed, slowly, the surface of the table. His hand identified Enid Bradley's wine glass; he did not knock it over. Then the box of ashes.

Taking an envelope out of his back pocket, he opened it and held it in one hand. With his other hand he opened the lid of the filigreed box.

He took a pinch of ashes out of the box and put it in the envelope. He closed the lid, sealed the envelope.

Turning, he walked into the chair in which Enid Bradley had sat that afternoon, talking to him. It moved only a few centimeters on the carpet.

When he slid the sliding door shut, the dog did not bark.

17

A gaggle of teen-aged girls joggled across Southworth Prep's green quadrangle in the bright Sunday morning sun. Fletch was waiting on the sidewalk outside an empty dormitory house.

As he came closer he saw the resemblance between the oldest girl, the only one not a teenager, and Enid Bradley—except that she was not at all overweight and her slit shorts and running shoes were not a bit out-of-date.

"Roberta?" he asked.

The girls were huffing along the sidewalk, pounding up the steps to the porch and into the house.

"Showers, everyone!" Roberta said. "Be ready for chapel in half an hour!"

She looked at Fletch.

"Roberta Bradley," Fletch said.

"Have we met?" she asked. She wasn't at all out of breath.

"We're just meeting now," Fletch said. "For probably the first and last time, no foolin'. I'm Fletcher."

"So?"

"I.M. Fletcher."

"You already said that."

"The jerk who wrote the piece in the newspaper Wednesday about Wagnall-Phipps."

"Oh, I see." Her look was not at all unfriendly. "You want to talk. It isn't necessary."

"I wanted to come by . . ."

She glanced at the clock in the church tower across the quadrangle. "I like to run another couple miles while the little darlings use up all the hot shower water. Mind running with me?"

"No. That's okay."

Her pace was faster than it had looked. She had long, skinny legs and a long stride. They got off the sidewalk and went behind the school buildings and along a dirt road.

"I run just to get a few minutes alone," she said.

"Sorry. Pretend I'm part of the landscape, if you want. Rock, tree, tumbleweed."

"The little darlings at Southworth Prep never give me time to go exercise Melanie. Dad's horse."

"You still keep your father's horse?"

Roberta ran silently for a minute or two. "Guess nobody's made a decision about it yet," she said. "Look, what do you want from me?"

"'Pologize, I guess. I screwed up. Must have been a shock to you."

Her face looked more annoyed than poised.

"Why is everybody making such a big deal of this? Wierder things have happened in the world. You wrote an article about Wagnall-Phipps and referred to my father as chairman. So what? You were just out of date, that's all."

"Still..."

"That three-piece suiter from the newspaper came over the other night, sat Tom and me down and gave us solemn apologies from the *News-Tribune*. Said mistakes happen. Don't you suppose we know mistakes happen? Jeepers!"

"It shouldn't have happened." Fletch's feet were raising bigger puffs of dirt than her's. "I hear Carradine had some nice things to say about me!"

Roberta smiled at him and waggled her head. "Boy, if you're half as bad as he says you are, you're awful! Incompetent, fool, compulsive liar, wow." She stretched her leg just slightly to avoid a rock embedded in the road. "Nice of you to come by, though, I suppose."

"I can't explain how it happened."

"No need to. You screwed up. So what? Last week I handed out a French test to a roomful of kids who were supposed to be taking a Spanish test. Would you believe two or three of the kids actually started to do the French test? No one should ever believe teachers or newspapers entirely."

"Your dad's dying in Switzerland and all.... Your mother taking over the company in his absence... then he died... your mother keeping the chair warm for your Aunt Francine...."

Roberta appeared to be listening carefully.

"There was some confusion," she said.

"Yeah. I guess you could say that."

"You can't understand everything that happens," Roberta said. "I tell that to my students. You can try to understand, of course. You can even act like you understand, when you don't yet. But some things..."

"What are you saying?"

"I hear jogging's good for the soul. Turns you philosophical."

"Especially on Sunday mornings."

"Here, we go back this way."

They ran together in silence for awhile.

"Nice of you to come by," she said again, finally. "There was no need to. Do you intend to see Tom, too?"

"Yes."

"I wish you wouldn't. He's busy with his pre-med studies, you know. What a grind! How that kid works! Let's just consider this incident closed. Okay?"

"Trying to do the decent thing."

"Well, you've done it." They were approaching the dormitory house. She said, "I'll be sure and tell Tom you stopped by." Then she said again, "Okay?"

Fletch said, "Was that really two miles we just ran?"

"Two measured miles. You can go around again, if you want."

They stopped in front of the house.

"No, thanks."

She was looking him over. "Looks like there's an envelope about to slip out of your pocket." She pointed to the back pocket of his jeans.

"Oh, that. Thanks." He slipped the sealed

envelope containing the ashes deeper into his pocket.

The house reverberated with giggles and shouts.

"Good thing you didn't lose it," she said. "You'd have to run around again to find it." She took the porch steps two at a time. "Thanks for coming by. I'll tell Tom."

"You want to see Tom?" The responsive, open face of Thomas Bradley Jr.'s college roommate was almost as wide as the dormitory room door he held open to Fletch. "He's here but he's gone."

At Fletch's puzzled expression, the roommate said, "We keep him in the bathtub."

He led Fletch around scrungy doorways to a scrungy bathroom.

In the bathtub, back and head resting on pillows, was a twenty-year-old man. His hair stuck up in stalks; his thin whiskers stood out from his chin and cheeks in patches, his eyes were closed. He looked a sad young man seriously contemplating the state of the universe.

"Figure he can't hurt himself so much in there. It's hard for him to get out. Hard for him to climb the sides, you know?"

"What's he on?"

"Downers, man. Downers all the way."

The roommate leaned over and opened one of Tom Bradley's eyes with his thumb. "Hello," he said. "Anybody home? Anybody in there?"

Fletch had told the roommate he had wanted to see Tom Bradley on *family business* and the roommate had said, *Somebody's come at last, thank God.*

121

"Hey, man," Fletch now said. "He can't live this way."

"Well, he does. Mostly. Sometimes he's cleaner than others. Gets up a bit, goes home, gets money. This is a new down."

"When did it start?"

"Friday. Two days ago. Was that Friday?"

"Shit. I was told he was a hard-working pre-med."

"Never was, really. He's always goofed. Came back to school last fall without much decision left. Attended classes irregularly a few weeks. Kept it up until, I guess, November—long after there was any reason to, he was so far behind already."

"So how come he's still living at the college?"

"What are we gonna do with him? Tried mailing him home, but the post office said he was too bulky a package. No, seriously. We carried him— physically carried him to the infirmary one night. Next day he was gone."

"When was that?"

"Way back before Christmas. Showed up here two weeks after New Year's all beat up. Looked like he had walked the jungles of Borneo. So we let him drive the bathtub some more. I went out to his house in Southworth—his mother's house. I told her she has a problem. Tom has a problem. At first, she looked frightened out of her wits. Then she denied everything I said. She said Tom shows up at the house every week or two, and I guess he does. She said he's just tired from his studies. Bullshit. Said he's been under heavy strain lately."

"What strain?" Fletch asked. "Did she say what strain?"

"Said something about his father's death."

"Supposedly that was a year ago."

Kneeling by the bathtub like a child playing with toy boats, the roommate looked up at Fletch. "Why do you say 'supposedly'?"

"He's got a pretty nice sister," Fletch said. "Healthy."

"Ta-ta? Yeah, I've talked to her, too."

"What does she say?"

"She says this is a world in which everybody's got to go for himself. She's a wind-up toy, and she thinks everybody else is, too. She says there's no understanding some things. There's no understanding her." Leaning over the tub side, the roommate slapped Tom Bradley's face a few times, lightly, until Tom opened his eyes. "Hey, Tom. Person to see you. Says his name is Satan. Wants to interview you for a job as a stoker."

Tom Bradley's glazed eyes were aimed at the ceiling. They darted to his roommate's face.

"Come on, Tom. You awake?"

Tom's eyes passed over Fletch and settled about a half meter to Fletch's left.

The roommate stood up. "Get somebody to do something about this kid, willya? I feel like someone who inherited an aquarium, you know? I have to take care of it and keep looking at it, when I'm not a whole lot interested, you know?"

"I don't know what I can do," said Fletch. "Not much, right away."

"Besides," the roommate said at the bathroom door. "I like to take a bath, you know?"

After Fletch heard the outer door close, he sat on the edge of the tub, near the faucet.

"Tom, people call me Fletch," he said. "I've

talked with your mother and your sister. Wanted to talk with you."

As Fletch had moved, Tom Bradley's eyes had remained looking a half meter to the left of Fletch's head.

"I wrote something about your father in the *News-Tribune* the other day. Some sort of a mistake. I don't know whether that's what's throwing you, or not. I suspect it didn't help any."

"My father?" Tom braced his neck against the back of the tub. His voice was louder than Fletch expected. "You going to tell me my father's dead again?"

"Hey, man."

"You talked to my father, lately?"

"Could I have?"

"Sure." Tom's smile came slowly, and his words were coming slowly. "Just go to the mantelpiece over the fireplace, open the little box, and say what you want to say. Or..." His unreal smile broadened. "You could use the telephone."

"Tom: is your father dead?"

"Sure." Again the response was overly loud. "Everybody says so. Even he says so."

"What's the joke, Tom? Come on, tell me."

After a long pause, Tom Bradley said, "My father's dead. He's worse than dead. You know?"

"No. I don't know. What's worse than dead?"

"He killed himself." Tom made the motion of sticking a knife into his stomach and rooting it around there.

"I see. He'd tried suicide before, hadn't he?"

Tom looked warily into the space beside Fletch's head.

"Tom, where did he die?"

"Southworth in the Spring. Vienna."

"France?"

"No. Not France."

"Switzerland?"

"Yeah. That's it. He died in Switzerland. Of blood cancer. Many, many operations."

"Okay, Tom. Why do you blame him for his death?"

Tom's eyes went around the small bathroom very, very slowly. "He didn't like."

Fletch waited until Tom's eyes settled back to the left of Fletch's head. "He didn't like what?"

Tom Bradley's eyes closed. "No. He didn't." Tom muttered, "That's the surprising thing, you see? Where does that leave me?"

"Where does that leave you?"

Tom's eyes opened, seemed to focus on the faucet between his legs, and closed again. He answered, "In the bathtub."

"Tom. One more question."

"I haven't heard any questions." With his eyes closed, Tom spoke more quickly.

"Where was your father born?"

"He wasn't. I guess he wasn't born. People only thought he was born."

"Where was he brought up?"

"In purgatory, he says. You know the word, purgatory?"

"Yeah."

"That's where he was brought up."

"In what town. What town is your father from, Tom?"

"Let me think."

Fletch waited until he believed Tom Bradley was gone into space again, and then stood up.

"Dallas, Texas," Tom Bradley then said.

For a moment, Fletch stood over him. Then he said, "Tom? Can you hear me?"

"No."

"Tom, I'm gonna try to help you. You don't need this thing—whatever it is. It might not look like I'm helping you. And it may even hurt. But I'm gonna try to help you."

After a while, Tom Bradley, Junior said, "Good bye."

"Later, Tom."

18

"Drink? Beer? Joint?"

Alston Chambers, law clerk in the District Attorney's office, took the five steps necessary to cross his livingroom and turned off the television set.

"Sunday afternoon," Fletch said. "Caught you sitting in front of the T.V. watching baseball and guzzling beer. Who'd ever think he'd live to see the day? Why aren't you out working around the palace? Painting, scraping, mowing and hoeing?"

Alston gave him a sardonic sideways glance. "Crappy little house. Who cares about it?"

"It's your mortgage, bud."

In the hot, dark livingroom an imitation early American divan, imitation Morris chair, pine wood coffee table, single standing lamp and ancient Zenith television left almost no place to stand. There was a bedroom in the house, and a kitchen-dinette. Houses each side were only a meter or so away, and there was a back yard big enough for the rubbish barrels.

"That's what it's all about," Alston said. "You don't buy a house. You buy a mortgage. I hate this house. I need the tax deduction. I need to establish credit. Everybody our age does. You, too, buddy. Wait till you get started. We're all waiting till you get started. Join the human race."

Clearly, Alston Chambers had joined the human race and clearly he was paying his dues. On a spring Sunday afternoon he was dressed in long trousers and moccasins and in his mid-twenties a beer belly made his dress shirt protrude and he was indoors drinking beer and looking at baseball on television. And since getting his law degree, he had been working nine-to-five as a clerk in the District Attorney's office.

Fletch and he had gone through Marine Corps basic training, and a great deal more, together.

"I would join the human race, Alston, honest, but something keeps going wrong. Everytime I apply, something happens. Some doggoned thing."

"You paying Linda her alimony like the judge told you to? Like a good boy?"

"No, sir."

Alston said, "I wouldn't expect anything else from you."

"Every month I sit down to write her a check, Alston, honest, but after the rent, the car payment, the utilities, the groceries..."

"There's nothing left. I know. I couldn't afford to pay alimony right now, either. You at least keeping up with your credit card payments?"

"I don't have any credit cards. I had one the

office gave me for, you know, expenses, but I lost that Thursday."

"What do you mean you lost it?"

"Well, it's more accurate to say I lost the use of it."

Alston looked at him incredulously. "You mean lost your job?"

"Or you could say I regained my freedom."

Alston chuckled. He turned around in the doorway and called his wife. "Audrey! Fletch is here."

"I'm just putting on a dress," she said through the wall. She sounded like she was in the room with them.

"Don't need to put on a dress for me, Audrey," Fletch said. "Wish you wouldn't."

"I know that, Fletch," she said, coming into the room and putting her arms around his neck. "But Alston's home, and we don't want to embarrass him, right?" She kissed him on the mouth.

"Right."

"Right," Alston said. "Now would you like a drink?"

He had picked up his pewter beer stein from the top of the television. Alston had bought the Austrian-style beer stein in Tokyo, Japan, when he and Fletch had been there on Rest and Recuperation.

"No, thanks." Audrey had sat on the divan. Fletch flopped into the single chair. "Moxie's got me going to this cocktail party at her theater tonight."

"Moxie?" Alston smiled down at him. "Is Moxie back on the scene?"

"Yeah. I guess so. Come to think of it, she is.

Bumped into her at a hot dog stand the other day. She's doing her thing—pretending that was the first time we ever met."

"That's Moxie," Alston said.

"That's Moxie."

"Did you say she's pretending you two just met for the first time, the other day?" Audrey laughed.

"Yeah. Come to think of it, she is."

"Moxie, Moxie," Alston said into his beer.

"Maybe it is the first time we ever met," Fletch said. "Moxie is a lot of different people, you know."

"All of them women," Alston said.

"Moxie's an actor," Fletch said, "whether she wants to be or not. She gets into an elevator and uses everybody else standing there as a captive audience. Once in a crowded elevator she turned to me and said, *Really, Jake, it hain't fair I got pregnant, when you said I wouldn't—you bein' my brother and all. What you go sayin' it wasn't possible for, when it was, alla time? You heard what the doctor just said— don't make no difference you bein' my brother. You tol' me a tootin' lie, Hank.*"

Laughing, Audrey said, "What did you do, Fletch?"

"Well, the temperature in the elevator went up to about one-hundred-and-thirty degrees fahrenheit. Every one was glowering at me. I wasn't sure I was going to get out of there alive."

"What did you do?" Audrey asked.

"I said, *Can't be sure it was me, Stella. Might ha' been Paw.*"

Alston slopped a little beer onto his shirt laughing.

"Was that the last time you two split?" Audrey asked.

Fletch thought a moment. "Time before that, I think. Last time, her father called from Melbourne, Australia, sobbing, saying he needed her to come play Ophelia, or he had to cancel the tour. She was packed and gone within fifteen minutes."

"I never knew Moxie played Ophelia in Australia," Audrey said.

"She didn't. She got there and the role had been filled. Freddy didn't even remember telephoning her. He said, *How nice of my little girl to come all this way to see her old daddy!* Something like that. Old bastard didn't even pay her way out, or back. She worked six months on a sheep ranch. Loved every minute of it. Said it was the best time of her life."

"So now she's pretending...what?" Audrey asked. "That you two never met before?"

"Yeah. She pretends we just met and then refers to a knowledge of me going back years. Sort of eerie."

"You two," Alston said. "Birds of a feather cluck together."

"You're both nuts," Audrey amplified. "Why don't you get married? I mean, neither of you should marry anyone else."

"Moxie will never marry," Fletch said. "She has this strange, necessary thing with being in love with whoever she's playing at the moment. Anyhow, she blames ol' Freddy for putting her mother in the hospital."

"Is she afraid she'll put you in the hospital?" Alston asked. "Fat chance."

"Making love to her has always been interesting," Fletch said. "You're never sure with whom you're making love."

Alston cleared his throat. "I think the two of you alone in a bedroom would make for quite a crowded room."

Fletch took the envelope out of his back pocket. "I came because I need a couple of favors."

"You name it," Alston said.

"There are some ashes in this envelope. I need them analysed chop-chop."

"Sure." Alston stepped over and took the envelope and put it in his own pocket.

"Second," Fletch said, "are you of sufficiently august rank in the District Attorney's office, Alston, to make a call to the United States Embassy in Geneva?"

"Never have done such a thing before," Alston answered. "Guess that's one of those things you do first and ask permission for second—Marine style."

"Good. I need the particulars on the death of an American citizen named Thomas Bradley. About a year ago. He may have died in hospital, or some kind of a special sanitorium. He may have committed suicide."

"From California?"

"Yes."

"You say about a year ago?"

"His widow says a year ago this month. His death was not announced here, though—or so it seems—until about six months later. The operation of a family business, Wagnall-Phipps; Bradley's wife running the company while she's waiting for someone else to take over—it's all mixed up some-how."

"How?"

Fletch said, "I don't know. I guess you could say: confusion has been caused, I suspect, deliberately."

"Suicide," Alston said. "You said the possibility of suicide. Isn't that enough of an explanation?"

"Not really."

"You'd be amazed," Alston said, "to know what my office still puts up with to permit people to conceal the fact of suicide. I don't disagree," he said. "I'm sympathetic. I go along with it."

Audrey said, "Alston, I think Fletch is considering the possibility of murder."

Alston looked at Fletch and Fletch continued looking at Audrey.

Alston said, "Are you, Fletch?"

"Suspicious death," Fletch said. "The guy may have died a year ago. But I suspect his kids weren't told until six months later. His neighbors and the president of the company he owned weren't told until eight months later. And, I have good reason to believe, his own Vice-president and treasurer wasn't told—really told—until last Thursday."

"It would be nice to have a look at the probate record," Alston said.

"Would there have to be one?"

"Sure. Property within the state . . ."

"Then I'd appreciate that, too."

"My fast answer is," Alston said, "really off the top of the head, is that somebody is trying to postpone, or evade altogether, death taxes, inheritance taxes. Was this a young guy?"

"Less than fifty."

"Death caught him with his pants down. In what kind of financial shape is this company of his, what's it called?"

"Wagnall-Phipps. I don't know."

"I suspect that's the answer," Alston said. "People don't expect to die so young. He died in Switzerland. Sounds to me like the estate's trying to take advantage of that fact to get the estate in shape, fiddle the taxes."

"I never thought of all that," Fletch said.

"You never went to Law School."

"Gee," Fletch said. "Is that why I haven't got either a mortgage or a credit card?"

"That's why," Alston said.

"I do have all those people called Moxie waiting for me." Fletch stood up. "Will tomorrow be too soon to call you, Alston?"

"Nope. I'll put highest priority on the chemical analyses, D.A. Demands, and I'll put in the call to Switzerland before I leave the house. Might even have the answers before noon. I'll call probate when I get to the office."

Audrey looked at him. "Don't you have anything else to do? I mean, any work of your own?"

"I seem to remember once or twice in the past Fletch dropping everything to help me," Alston said. "In case I haven't mentioned this before, Audrey, I wasn't a very with-it Marine."

"Bye, Fletch." She kissed him on the cheek. "Thanks for saving my husband's ass."

"Hell with his ass," Fletch said. "It's his sense of humor I saved."

On the sidewalk in front of the house, Alston Chambers said, "Fletch, I've got a bank balance of over five hundred dollars. All or part of it are yours, any time you want it."

"Poo!" Fletch said. "What's money? Tissue paper! Who needs it?"

Sitting in the car, Fletch said through the window, "Thanks, Alston. Call you tomorrow."

19

"Shit on a windy corner!" Moxie muttered as she got into the passenger seat of the car in the dark. "You even beat Freddy Mooney!"

"Don't bother giving me directions. I know where the Colloquial Theater is."

"I never in my life came across such a wierd man as you are!"

"Across the bridge, right?"

She didn't even glance in the direction they were going.

"I mean, my God! In the three days I've known you all you've done is cry poor. Poor me! I've lost my job, wail, wail, wail! You haven't bought me any food in three days!"

"Orange juice. I bought the orange juice."

"I put my name on the dotted line for a steak, pal. And a bottle of wine. Had to pretend I was a bride new to the neighborhood with a husband working in a bank."

"You're good that way."

"You've got fifty dollars—I've got about the same, for the rest of my life." Even to Fletch her imitation of him sounded accurate. "You leave the house to run around the countryside in your sports car." She slapped the dashboard of the M.G. with her hand. "I spot a wallet hanging out of your dirty jeans, say, *What's this?*, pull it out, open it up, and there—right there before my eyes as surprising as Mount Everest in the Sahara Desert—is twenty-five thousand dollars cash in one thousand dollar bills!"

"It's not my money, Moxie. I told you that, at the apartment."

"You wouldn't even buy us lunch with a credit card!"

"I told you. The money belongs to James St. E. Crandall."

"Losers weepers!"

"Twenty-five thousand dollars worth of weepers?"

"Mister Fletcher, may I point out to you that anyone who can drop twenty-five thousand dollars cash on the sidewalk and not even look around is also someone who knows where his next poached egg is coming from?"

"I don't know that. Neither do you."

"I do know, on the other hand, that you do not know where your next poached egg is coming from."

"That has nothing to do with it."

"That's why you drove about one-hundred-and-fifty miles out of your way to stop at that dead-water town, Worrybeads, or whatever it was, right?"

"Wramrud."

"Whatever. Here's a guy trying to give away twenty-five thousand dollars in cash while he's starving. I ask you, is that sensible?"

"I'm not starving."

"You never even mentioned you were carrying so much money. And there we were, sleeping on a beach!"

"That was nice. And I did, too, mention it."

"Yeah. *So I took the twenty-five thousand dollars.* That's what you said. Is everything you say a joke? Are you a joke, Irwin Fletcher?"

Going onto the bridge Fletch's eye caught something fluttering in the breeze, a piece of cloth, to his right, half-way across.

"You sound like a wife," he said.

She grinned across at him, her face picking up the light from the dashboard. "Hoped you'd say that. I rehearsed."

He was slowing the car.

It was a skirt that was fluttering in the breeze. Fletch could see one leg below it, very white, and above it, hanging onto a bridge cable, an arm.

He pulled the car's hazard lights switch, and pulled over to the right as far as he could.

"Get out of the car, Moxie, and stand as much out of the way as you can. Don't stand in front of the car."

"You're stopping in the middle of the bridge?"

"That's why you're getting out and standing as much out of the way as you can. The car might get hit."

"What's the matter?"

"Be right back."

Fletch got out of the car and ran back along the bridge. He saw one of the cars approaching him was a taxi. He stood in front of the taxi, making it stop.

"Bastard! You crazy?" the taxi driver shouted through his window. "Son-of-a-bitch! You some kind of a nut?"

Fletch leaned through the window. "You got a radio-phone? C.B.?"

"Yeah. What are you?"

"Call the cops," Fletch said. "Jumper."

"Yeah. Oh, yeah." The taxi driver reached for the microphone hanging from his dashboard. "Where?"

"There." Fletch waved his arm toward the edge of the bridge and then pointed to his own car. "Pull your car behind mine, will you? You got bigger lights. A roof light."

"Yeah. Sure."

The car rolled forward. "You goin' out there?"

"Near enough to talk, I guess."

"Jeez. Crazy bastard."

Fletch watched the taxi, its roof light on, its hazard lights flashing, stop behind his car. Moxie's face looked white in the headlights of the taxi.

Then Fletch stepped onto the knee-high guard rail. Looking down he saw the lower ledge of the I-beam and stepped down onto it. From there he saw the river far, far below him, some lights, moonlight, city lights, bridge lights, reflecting off, wavering on the oiley, sluggish water. He tried to decide the water was too far away for him to care about it.

There was an L-shaped strut extending away

from the bridge to a cable running parallel with the bridge road. The cable was as thick as a sewer pipe. He put one foot on the strut. There was not much wind, but there was some. He looked at the woman who was standing further along the cable, over the water to his right. There was enough wind to make her skirt flutter and stand out.

"Fletch?" Moxie's voice came from behind him. Her voice sounded sincerely inquiring, as if she were about to ask him a question,

Both of Fletch's feet were on the strut. He stood up straight, his hands free in the air. Then purposely fell forward, grabbing the cable with both arms, hugging it.

He held on a moment, his cheek against the cable's fabric.

"Fletch?" Moxie said. "I think I'll shut my face, now."

Fletch pulled himself more onto the cable, pulled his hips onto it. His empty stomach sent an inquiry to his brain regarding the dark water swirling far below him. He pulled his feet closer to the cable and putting weight on them, on the strut, flipped himself over. For a second, neither foot, neither hand was on anything.

Then he was sitting up, his feet on the strut, his hands on the cable each side of him, the breeze in his face. On the bridge, car horns were complaining about the two parked cars. Moxie and the taxi driver, facing him, were in silhouette.

To Fletch the woman standing to his left on the cable still appeared mostly as a fluttering skirt. She was wearing one green, plastic, ballet-style slipper. The other slipper was gone. Her legs were white and heavy and broken with varicose veins.

Easily, Fletch said, "Hi."

The woman's head turned. Two large, dark eyes stared down at him from deep, hollow sockets. Thick black hair waved around her face.

"What do you like?" Fletch asked.

She stared down at him.

"Do you like chocolate?"

She turned her head back into the wind, the dark, back into space, and said something.

"What?" Fletch asked. "I didn't hear you."

She turned her head back to him, annoyed.

"What do you like?" she asked. "Tell me that."

"I like chocolate," Fletch said. "I like to see birds hopping on the grass. Do you like to see little birds hopping on the green grass?"

She said something that was lost in the wind.

"What else do you like?" Fletch asked. "Who do you like on television?"

There was no answer.

"Mike Wallace? Merv Griffin? How about *As The World Turns*? Do you ever watch that?"

No answer.

Fletch's throat was dry.

"Hey," he said, "do you remember the smell of a brand new car? Really new?"

No answer.

"How about the smell of brownies baking? Isn't that the greatest?"

From above she was staring down at him.

"What kind of sounds do you like?" he asked. "Harmonica? Violin? Guitar?"

No answer.

"You know what I like?" he asked. "I love seeing a newspaper page blowing along a city street. I love to hear rain—really hard rain—when I'm in bed. The yap of a puppy. Do you like to hear the yap of a puppy sometimes?"

"Hey," the woman said. "Kid."

"Yeah?"

"Take my hand, willya? I'm scared shitless."

"So am I," Fletch said.

She began reaching for him, immediately tottering.

"Wait a minute," Fletch said. "There has to be a right way to do this."

To sidle toward her, Fletch would have to take his feet off the strut.

"Just sit down," Fletch said. "Right where you are. Slowly, carefully."

Slowly, carefully she sat down on the cable, facing the bridge. The green plastic slipper dangled from her foot.

"Hold onto me," she said.

Fletch took her hand.

"Wait for the cops," Fletch said. "We'll wait for the cops."

"What the fuck we doing out here?" the woman asked.

"I don't know," he answered. "Sometimes we find ourselves places like this."

She was shivering then. "It's not my fault, you know. It really isn't."

"I'm sure it isn't," Fletch said. "Tell me what you like. What's the nicest book you ever read?"

"That's a funny question."

"Well, what is the nicest book you ever read?"

"*Black Beauty*," the woman said.

"Tell me about it."

The woman thought a moment. "I don't remember nothin' about it," she said, "'cept that I liked it."

"Hey, great," Fletch said. "You get to read it again."

"This really isn't my fault," the woman said. "Believe me."

"I believe you," Fletch said. "Believe me I believe you."

And there came onto the bridge the swirling lights of two police cars, then a fire truck, then the Rescue Squad truck. A policeman and then a fireman had spoken to Moxie and the taxi driver.

The man in the fire hat called to Fletch and the woman. "All right to come over?"

"Sure," Fletch answered.

"All right," the woman said.

A canvas-backed ladder was run across to them, landing on the cable between them, and a fireman walked across on it and took the woman by the arms and helped her to stand up. He guided her feet on the ladder, putting himself behind her, holding her arms, bearing most of her weight himself, urging her to move her feet along. From behind he looked a giant child walking a rag doll.

Halfway across, the fireman turned his head back to Fletch. "Want me to come back for you?"

"Just give me a minute," Fletch said. "I'll be right there. Put the coffee pot on."

Once the woman and the fireman were off the ladder, Fletch crawled along it back to the bridge on all fours.

20

"Really, Moxie," said the theater Director in the light-weight, double-breasted blazer, "this does not bode well. If you're so late showing up for a cocktail party, how can I expect you to show up on time for rehearsals and performances?"

"We got held up on the bridge," Fletch said.

"Everyone gets held up by a bridge," the Director said. "That's what bridges do."

"We were delayed on the bridge," Moxie said.

The Colloquial, like most theaters not putting on an illusion at that moment, looked a cross between a dirty warehouse and an impoverished church. On one side of the stage, lumber was stacked. On the other side, a long, flimsy table held half-eaten wheels of cheese and many empty wine bottles. Out front were rows of dispirited, sagging chairs, existentially weary of tears and laughter, tragedy and comedy.

When Moxie and Fletch had entered the stage from the wings other members of the cast and crew summed up Moxie coolly, professionally watching the way she walked and stood. None evinced a more human interest in her. Only the Director had come forward to greet her.

"At least you're alive," the Director said. "And you're here. We must be grateful for small favors."

"And I've studied the *In Love* script," Moxie said in a small voice. "Paul, I think it's wonderful."

"You'll meet the author tomorrow, I trust," the Director said. "He flew in from New York this afternoon and was just too exhausted to stand up, he said. I suspect the truth is he intends to use his time out here trying to get a paying job in television." The Director elevated his eyebrows at Fletch. "Is this the boy you wanted me to meet?"

"This is Fletch," Moxie said. "You said on the phone you're not all that keen on Sam..."

The Director stood back, eyebrows still half way up his forehead, and looked Fletch up and down and up again, as if to gauge his suit size.

"Nice looking," the Director said. "Natural. I suppose your bodies would work well together."

"They do," commented Fletch.

"How do you feel about being naked?" the Director asked.

Fletch answered, "I was born that way."

"But you weren't born on a stage," the Director said. "Although, of course, Moxie was. How is dear Freddy Mooney, Moxie, your inveterate Pa?"

"Inveterate, thank you."

"But, my God, doesn't he bathe?" the Director said of Fletch. "I mean, I know dirt turns some people on, but not enough of them to fill a theater at these prices."

"Am I dirty?" Fletch asked Moxie.

"Grimey," Moxie said. "Streaked."

"I'll swear I took a shower in the fall."

"He's really as clean as a whistle, usually," Moxie said. "It's just that, on the way over, he..."

"He what?" asked the Director. "Did the backstroke through the city dump?"

"He saved a woman's life," Moxie said. "Sweaty work, that."

"But can he act?" the Director asked.

"No," Fletch said. "Not at all."

"How refreshing of you to say that. Finally, in California, I've heard a new line: No, I can't act. If you're seriously applying for the male lead in *In Love*, Mister Fletch, or whatever your name is, you must know you have to appear nude on stage not once, but twice. I'll see to it that you take a shower before each performance. Afterward, you're on your own."

Fletch turned to Moxie and asked, in a reasonable tone, "Moxie, darling, what are you doing?"

"Tell him what a great actor you are, Fletch."

"I can't act at all."

"Nonsense," said Moxie, "you've been acting all your life."

"Never."

"You need the job, Fletch."

"Not a job acting."

"It would be fun," Moxie said. "You and me."

"It would be horrible."

"You don't have anything else to do."

"In fact, I do have something else to do."

"What? Interview more dead people?"

"Moxie?"

"Anyway," the Director said, "you should meet Sam, Moxie. Your present male lead. Tell me what you think of him. Oh, Sam!" the Director called.

Across the stage a dark-haired, heavy-browed young man stood up from a pile of lumber and started to walk over.

"Ape," the Director said quietly. "He walks like an orangutan with gonorrhea. Heavy thighs. Today's audiences do not like heavy thighs. Oh, Sam, meet Moxie Mooney."

"Hullo," Sam said.

"Hullo," said Moxie.

"Why don't you two children greet each other with a kiss? You'll be working together."

Both Moxie and Sam put their faces forward to be kissed, neither to kiss. After indecisive, awkward maneuvers, the kiss was perfunctory.

"Theater history is made," said the Director sardonically.

"It will be nice working with you, I'm sure," Moxie said.

"Yeah," Sam said. "I saw your dad play *King Lear.* Is it true he once ran a carnival knife-throwing act?"

Moxie's eyes became slits.

"Instant electricity," the Director said. "Serendipity. I must rush home and get it all down in my journal, for posterity."

"See you," Sam said.

"Ten a.m.," said the Director.

Sam ambled off-stage through the scenery.

The Director sighed. "What do you think?" he asked Moxie.

"I don't think," Moxie said. "I act."

"At least you have the sense to realize it, dear. I wish other actors wouldn't think they could think. Listen," the Director said to Fletch. "Hang loose a few days. I don't think Sam is going to work out. I hate to fire someone for thick thighs—"

"What?" Fletch said. "No."

"Okay," Moxie said. "He will."

"I can see you two as much more of a team. I mean, you'd be beautiful together, if one of you would take a shower. Really exciting to watch."

"I'm sorry to come to your party with a dirty face," Fletch said.

"Dirt can have its charms," the Director said. "Especially when used to grow tulips."

"May we go now, Moxie?"

"We just got here. I haven't met the crew."

"I need a shower."

"He does need a shower, Moxie. You can meet the rest of the cast in the morning. Do try to be here at ten A.M. Excuses will not be tolerated." The Director pointed at Fletch. "Take this boy home and wash him!"

21

"I've done you a favor," Moxie said a few times during the evening.

In bed, after they'd showered, after they'd eaten peanut butter sandwiches, after Fletch had explained to Moxie again he had no intention of trying to be an actor and she had explained to him, again, patiently, that, yes, he would so try, that doubtlessly he would be far better than Sam in the role, Fletch's legs were straighter, and after they, again, physically penetrated who each other were at that moment, lying back in the dark room, Moxie asked, "Fletcher?"

"Yes, Ma'm?"

"Where were you this morning?"

"When this morning?"

"I woke up at three o'clock. You weren't in bed. You weren't in the bathroom. You weren't in the apartment at all."

"I went out to do a spot of housebreaking."

"Jeez," Moxie said. "The way you say things I'd almost believe it. Not an actor, uh?"

"Not to worry. I got away with it."

"Well." She contracted and expanded, put her arm and her leg on his, so she'd be more comfortable. "I've done you a favor. A thousand-dollar favor. Or, a twenty-four thousand dollar favor, depending on your point of view."

"How's that again?"

"I've stolen a thousand dollars from you. From the wallet."

"What? What do you mean?"

"Well, it makes sense, Fletch. You're not spending the money when you really need to because you want to be able to return the whole twenty-five thousand dollars to the man. Right?"

"Right."

"Well, now you can't return the whole twenty-five thousand dollars to the man. Because I've got a thousand dollars of it. So you might as well do the sensible thing and spend the rest of the money yourself. Right?"

"Are you serious?"

"As serious as a flash flood in Abu Zabi."

"Perverted."

"What?"

"Perverted reasoning."

"Hardly."

"Moxie, you've stolen a thousand dollars which doesn't belong to me."

"Right. Thus giving you use of twenty-four thousand dollars."

"That's corrupt. You're a crook."

"I'm a sensible, clever lady."

"What have you done with the money?"

"Hidden it."

"Where?"

"Some place you'll never find it."

"Where would that be?"

"That's for me to know and for you not to find out."

"You're serious about this."

"Entirely."

"Do you intend to spend the money?"

"I will if I want. If there's something I want that costs a thousand dollars, I'll spend it."

"Is there something you want that costs a thousand dollars?"

"Not that I know of. Probably I'll think of something. I didn't really steal the money to spend it."

"Oh, no. Of course I believe that."

"You make me sound like a suspicious person."

"You're not suspicious. You're a crook."

"Fletcher, if you'd lost twenty-five thousand dollars in cash, do you think anyone else would drive all around the country trying to get it back to you?"

"I certainly hope so."

"Than you're an idealist slightly more demented than Icarus."

"Which Icarus is that?"

"The guy who flew toward the sun with wings attached by wax. The melting kind of wax."

"Oh, that Icarus. That kind of wax."

"Demented."

"Moxie, there's such a thing as a social contract. It makes the world go 'round."

"I don't notice Frank Jaffe, or your newspaper, observing any social contract with you."

"Of course they have. It appears I goofed, and they fired me. That's perfectly agreeable."

"You were lied to by someone at Wagnall-Phipps."

"Charles Blaine. And Enid Bradley did try to observe the social contract with me. She offered me money to make up for the damage I've suffered at the hands of Wagnall-Phipps."

"Did you accept?"

"No."

"More likely she offered you money to make you go away."

"I think so, too."

"It's also written into the social contract, Loosers weepers, Finders keepers."

"Where is that written?"

"Page 38. Clause 74."

"That's the social contract for young readers. Ages four to seven."

"Really, Fletch."

"Moxie, what am I going to do if I find the man, this James St. E. Crandall, and I haven't got the full twenty-five thousand dollars?"

"I have just given you reason—necessity, you might call it—to stop looking for James St. E. Crandall. Don't you get the point? You're such a slow boy."

"You're a crook. You've stolen a thousand dollars."

"I've done you a favor."

"Stop doing me favors. At seven o'clock you're doing me the favor of trying to get me a job as a male stripper. At eleven o'clock you tell me you've done me the favor of stealing a thousand dollars from me. What's the next favor you're going to do me? Give me whooping cough?"

"I'll think about it."

"Jeez!"

"You think about it, too."

"Think about what?"

"All the nice favors I've been doing you. You'll feel much better in the morning. You'll wake up and realize you have twenty-four thousand dollars to spend. You're so rich you can even afford to work in the theater."

"Good night, darling."

"'Night, lover. Sweet dreams."

22

Fletch opened his apartment door to the corridor and found himself looking down at himself, his face streaked with grime and sweat, on the front page of the *News-Tribune*.

"Oh, no."

MOTORIST PREVENTS BRIDGE SUICIDE ATTEMPT
was the headline over the photograph.

Towel wrapped around his waist, he picked up the newspaper, closed the door, and sat down on the divan in his livingroom.

An observant passerby with a willingness to risk his life to save the life of another climbed out onto the superstructure of the Guilden Street Bridge after dark last night and talked a middle-aged female potential suicide victim back to safety.

"In this life we're all in the same car together," said Irwin Maurice Fletcher, 24.

Until Friday of last week, Fletcher was a member of the News-Tribune *editorial staff.*

Fletcher said his eye happened to be caught by the potential victim's skirt fluttering in the breeze as he drove onto the bridge...

The telephone rang. Absently, still reading, Fletch picked up the receiver.

"Hello?"

"Fletch? Janey. Frank wants to talk to you."

"Frank who?"

"Hey, Fletch!" Frank Jaffe's voice sounded too cheery for a Monday morning. "You made the front page."

"Not the first time, Esteemed Managing Editor."

"The *News-Tribune* gave you quite a spread."

"I have it in my lap. Nice of you guys to report in the third paragraph you fired me last week. Really helps in the care and feeding of Irwin Maurice Fletcher."

"Makes us look like shits, don't it?"

"It do."

"Had to report it. Journalistic honesty, you know?"

"You had to report it in the lead?"

"Yeah, well, I agree—that stinks. Some of the people around here are pretty burned off at you, in case I didn't tell you before. One old desk man wondered aloud this morning why you didn't let the woman jump so you could then interview her. After she drowned, that is."

"I got the point, Frank."

"Some of these guys have a truly vicious sense of humor."

"Tell them if they don't restrain themselves I won't interview them after they're dead."

"I don't suppose you want to hear the head-line they really wanted to run."

"I don't suppose I do."

"You might."

"I doubt it."

"I mean, with your irrepressible sense of hu-mor?"

"Okay, Frank. Give it to me. I haven't had breakfast yet."

"The headline they wanted to run was GUILDEN STREET BRIDGE HERO FIRED BY THE NEWSPAPER YOU TRUST."

"Too long for a headline. Why did you call, Frank. To congratulate me?"

"Hell, no. I've always known you could talk the bark off a tree. No big feat, talking a woman off a bridge. Not for you."

"So why did you call?"

"It's Monday morning. I'm in the office."

"So?"

"You said I wouldn't be. You cast aspersions at Clara Snow's cooking."

"You must have a goat's stomach, Frank. I know you've got his horns."

"Actually, I was thinking, Fletch."

"I can smell the smoke."

"You write pretty well."

"When I have a chance."

"You have the chance. I'm giving it to you. What I'm thinking is, this is a perfect opportunity for a first-hand account, you know? Big feature."

"You mean, like, HOW I TALKED THE SUICIDE OFF THE BRIDGE BY I.M. FLETCHER?"

"You got it."

"No, thanks, Frank."

"Why not? You got something else to do to-day?"

"Yes. I have."

"We'll pay you. Guest writer's rates."

Guest writer's rates were on the lower side of adequate.

"Gee, thanks, Frank. But I don't work for you anymore, remember?"

"Might clean up your reputation a little."

"Might sell you a few newspapers."

"That, too."

"Know what, Frank? You're not a bad managing editor—even if you are burying that story about the Governor's Press Secretary's brother selling cars to the state police."

"Know what, Fletch? You're not a bad kid—even if you do interview dead people."

"See you, Frank."

"See you, Fletch."

When Moxie came into the livingroom, she looked at the newspaper and said, "You're not twenty-four."

Still sitting on the divan, Fletch shook his head sadly. "Goes to show you. You should never believe everything you read in a newspaper." He looked up at her, dressed only in his old, torn denim shirt. "Come on. Get dressed. I'll drive you to the theater."

"Where's breakfast?" she asked.

"Same place that thousand dollar bill is, you stole from the wallet yesterday."

She looked at him sharply. "Where's that?"

He shrugged. "I wish I knew."

23

"Are you the manager of this bank?" Fletch asked the skinny man in a worn out suit who sat at a big desk the other side of a railing.

"Indeed I am." The man smiled at him warmly. "You look like someone who could use a car loan. We can do very well for you on a car loan."

"No, thanks. I have a car loan." Fletch waved a thousand dollar bill. "I want to know if this is real."

The manager saw the bill and gestured Fletch around the railing to his desk. The manager took the bill in the fingers of both hands and felt it as would a clothing merchant feeling material. He examined it closely through his eye-glasses. Especially did he examine closely the engraving of Grover Cleveland.

"Do you have any reason to doubt its authenticity?" the manager asked.

"Sure. I've never seen one before."

"You don't see too many pictures of Grover Cleveland."

"Is that who it is? I thought it might be Karl Marx."

The manager looked at him in shock. "Karl Marx?"

Fletch shrugged. "Don't see too many pictures of him, either."

The manager chuckled. "It looks okay to me."

"Will you cash it for me?"

"Sure."

Fletch took another thousand dollar bill out of the pocket of his jeans. "This one, too?"

The manager examined the second thousand dollar bill even more closely. "Where did you get these?"

"My employer is a little eccentric. Hates to write checks."

"You must be well paid." The manager looked closely at Fletch. "I've seen you somewhere before."

"Have you?"

"Your picture. I've seen your picture—very recently."

"Oh, that," said Fletch. "I'm on the five-thousand dollar bill."

"Maybe on a Wanted Poster?" The skinny man laughed. "How do you want these bills broken up?"

"Hundreds, fifties, twenties, tens, fives."

The manager stood up. "You just want it spendable, right?"

"Right."

"I'll be right back."

The fistfulls of money the manager brought back to Fletch were bigger than Fletch expected. The manager counted it out again, on the desk in front of Fletch.

"Thank you." Fletch was having difficulty stuffing the bills into the pockets of his jeans.

"I'm just slightly uneasy." The manager looked closely again at Fletch's face. "I've seen a picture of you somewhere—I think, this morning."

"Did you read the funnies?"

"Yes," the manager answered. "I read the funnies on the bus."

Fletch said, "That must be it, then."

"When will the suit be ready?"

"Ten days."

"Not soon enough."

"When do you need it?"

"Wednesday."

"This is Monday."

"Thursday morning then."

"We'll see what we can do."

Besides the well-cut, serious blue business suit, Fletch had bought, in the very expensive men's shop, shirts, shoes, neck-ties, tennis sneakers, shorts, sport shirts, and, a suitcase.

"Going on a vacation?" the salesman asked.

"Yes," answered Fletch. "I'd like to take everything with me, except the suit."

"Certainly, Mister Fletcher. How do you choose to pay? We'll accept your check."

"Cash." Fletch took a mess of bills from the pocket of his jeans.

"Very good, sir. I'll have everything wrapped for you."

"No need. I'll just put everything in the suit-case."

"If that's what you wish."

While the salesman added up the bill and made change, Fletch packed the suitcase.

"Mister Fletcher," the salesman said slowly. "I wonder if you'd accept a gift from the store."

"A gift?"

"That was quite a wonderful thing you did last night—taking that woman off the bridge."

"You know about that?"

"Everyone knows about that." The salesman's eyes studied the deep carpeting. "Our cashier, last year, found herself in similar straits. You see, no one knew, understood..."

"So people do read newspapers."

"We're proud to have you a customer of our store."

Other salespersons, Fletch now noticed, were standing around watching him.

The salesman handed Fletch a boxed silver-backed brush and comb.

"Wow," said Fletch.

"They're made in England," the salesman said.

"Real nice." Fletch shook the salesman's hand. "Real nice of you."

"People make efforts so seldom for other people..." The salesman seemed embarrassed.

"Thank you," said Fletch.

With suitcase in one hand and the boxed brush and comb in the other, Fletch proceeded to leave the store.

All the salespersons smiled at him as he went by, and applauded him.

"You don't want to go to San Orlando," the heavily made-up woman in the tight-fitting jacket said. On the wall of the travel agency posters recommended Acapulco, Athens, Nice, Naples, Edinburgh, Amsterdam, and Rio de Janiero. Fletch wanted to go to all of them.

"I must," Fletch said.

"No one *must* go to San Orlando." She had the phone to her ear, waiting for information from the airline. "You know where Puerto de San Orlando is? Way down the Mexican coast. Takes forever to get there. They haven't finished building it yet. Barely started. One hotel. The place is insuperably hot, dusty—hello?" She noted information from the airline. "That's terrible," she said, hanging up. "Terrible connections all the way through. It's a far more expensive trip than it's worth, at this point. If you waited a few years, until after they've developed the place a little..."

Leaning on the counter she told Fletch about the bad connections to San Orlando, and the expense.

"Fine," said Fletch. "Reservations for one, please."

"For one?" The woman looked truly shocked.

"One," Fletch said.

"Boy," the woman said. "Is being a hero *that* bad?" She sat down at the small desk behind the counter. "Return when?"

"Wednesday."

"Wednesday? This is Monday."

"Got to pick up a new suit," Fletch said. "Thursday morning."

She put the airline's ticket form into the type-writer. "Some people's idea of fun. It's all right, I suppose, as long as they have the travel agent to blame."

24

"Hey, Fletch!" Alston Chambers said, answering the phone to him. "You're an unemployed hero again!"

In his apartment, sitting on the divan, Fletch put his coffee mug precisely over his own mug on the front page of the *News-Tribune*. Moxie had left the newspaper on the coffee table.

"I'm beginning to think that's your natural condition," Alston said. "Heroically unemployed."

"Aw, shucks. 'Twarn't nothin'."

"I wouldn't have gone out on that bridge cable for a million dollars. A million plus lose change. Especially in the dark."

"Actually, I never did decide to do it, Alston. I just did it."

"It's a good thing you're thoughtless, Fletch."

"Am I calling too early?" Fletch's watch read two thirty.

"Nope. I called the U.S. Embassy in Geneva before I left home, and they answered here at the office before noon. Was the name you gave me Thomas Bradley spelled B-r-a-d-l-e-y?"

"Yeah."

"No American citizen named Thomas Bradley has died in Switzerland."

"Ever?"

"Ever."

"No Thomas Bradley has ever died in Switzerland?" Fletch admired his new suitcase standing on the floor just inside the apartment's front door. "Do they know about deaths in private sanitoriums?"

"They say they do. They assure me their records regarding in-country deaths are one hundred percent accurate. I should think they would be."

"Even if the guy was cremated?"

"I asked them to check deaths and burials, removals, what have you, under all circumstances. Swiss paperwork, you know, leaves the rest of the world blushing. Wherever your man died, it wasn't Switzerland. Did you hear the announcement on the noon news the mayor is giving you The Good Citizen of The Month Citation?"

"The month isn't over yet. What about the ashes I gave you, Alston?"

"Oh, yeah. I dropped them at the police lab on my way to work. Why did you give them to me, anyway?"

"What was the result?"

"The result was that the good gentlemen in white coats called when I got back from lunch and asked if the D.A. had really wanted those ashes

analysed. I assured the gentleman solemnly that
the D.A. did. I didn't tell him that by 'D.A.' I
meant a damned ass named Fletch."

"Alston—"

"Carpet."

"What?"

"Carpet. You know, rug? They were the ashes
of a tightly woven, high quality carpet. Probably
Persian."

"A carpet?"

"A quantity of petroleum, it says here, probably kerosene, a few wood ashes, probably pine,
and a small measure of earth and sand."

"Are those guys always right?"

"Listen, Fletch, these guys do the lab work for
every suspected arson in the state. They know a
burned rug when they see one. They were very
curious as to which case of arson we're working
on. By the way, Fletch, which case of arson are we
working on?"

"None I know of."

"Is Moxie burning up the family heirlooms so
she can get a job playing in *Die Walkure*?"

"Something like that."

"Fletch, was Audrey right?"

"Probably. About what?"

"Are you on to a murder?"

"I don't know that at this point."

"What do you know at this point?"

"At this point..." Fletch thought a moment.
"...I know Thomas Bradley was a carpet."

> *Dear Moxie,*
> *Gone to Mexico to see a man about a carpet.*
> *Try to manage dinner by yourself. If you take anything*

from the refrigerator, please leave a $1,000 bill in the ice tray. Probably I'll be back Wednesday night.

—F.

25

In late morning the sun on the Pacific Ocean and on the white sand of the beach at San Orlando was dazzling, dizzying to anyone who had spent most of the previous night jack-rabbiting in airplanes. Fletch had arrived at the hotel at two forty five A.M., discovered there was nothing for him to eat, slept for three hours, awoke too hungry to sleep more, swam in the hotel pool until the breakfast room opened at seven, ate steak, eggs, bacon, homefries and fried tomatoes, then went out to the beach and fell asleep again.

The travel agent had been right. The airline's connections had been terrible: three different flights, each with a wait longer than the flight. She had been right that Puerto de San Orlando was just beginning to be built: whole walls were missing from the hotel; the landscaping was typified by weeds growing through cement blocks; beaten paths led from decorated bar to diningroom to pool. The sounds of bulldozers grinding, hammers bamming, saws buzzing filled the dusty air. She also had been right about Puerto de San Orlando's insuperable heat.

Late morning, Fletch took a table for two in the palm-roofed, open-sided bar on the beach and ordered a beer. Hot though he was, the beer was not cold. His eyes stung from the three jet airplane hops during the night, the brilliant sunlight reflected from the ocean and the beach, from swimming in the salt water. He drank his beer slowly and then ordered a Coca Cola. The Coke wasn't cold, either.

Just before noon he saw Charles Blaine, in long plaid shorts and a yellow sports shirt, heavy horn-rimmed glasses and sandals, come through the hotel's arched doorway and plod across the sand to the beach bar.

When Blaine came into the shade of the palm-leaf roof he stopped, looked around. His eyes passed over Fletch, sitting at the table in just swimming trunks, blinked, and looked back. Blaine frowned like an accountant spotting red ink on books he had felt were not perfectly sound. He turned to go, apparently thought better of it, looked again at Fletch, hesitated, and then walked over to Fletch's table.

"You'd make a good accountant," Charles Blaine said to Fletch. "You don't give up."

Fletch turned his head toward the sea. "I'd make a good reporter, too. Pity I can't get a job as either."

Blaine put his hand on the other chair. "Shall I sit down?"

"I didn't come to Puerto de San Orlando," Fletch said slowly, "to drink the water."

Blaine sat down.

"Drink?" Fletch asked. "Warm beer or warm Coke?"

"Gin and tonic."

"Sounds good," Fletch said. "Me, too."

"Mexico has excellent limes," Blaine advised.

"I should think so."

They ordered from the young waitress whose hips were stacked on her like lava flow on a volcanic mountain.

"Nice vacation?" Fletch asked Blaine.

"Yes, thank you."

"Sort of an out-of-the-way place you chose for a vacation."

"It's not too expensive—once you get here." Charles Blaine then listed the exact price of everything purchaseable in Puerto de San Orlando, Mexico, in both pesos and dollars—every article of food, drink, clothing, every souvenir.

Fletch asked, "How's your nervous breakdown doing?"

"Am I having one?"

"Enid Bradley says so."

"Does she? One of us may be having a nervous breakdown—either Enid or myself."

"She says you are. She says you were so fond of her husband you can't let him rest in peace. You can't believe he's dead. You keep referring to him in the present tense."

"Me, fond of Thomas Bradley?"

"Weren't you?"

"Thomas Bradley was my boss. I was as fond of him as I am of my desk, chair, filing cabinet, and desk calculator. He was a necessary piece of office equipment. As replaceable in my life as any other boss."

"There's some evidence," Fletch said, "that you're so eager to perpetuate the myth that Thomas Bradley is still alive that you even go so far as to forge memos from him."

A small, quirky smile flashed on Blaine's face.

"Why did you come here, Fletcher? What's your question?"

Fletcher looked innocently at Charles Blaine. "Was Thomas Bradley really a carpet?"

Blaine's eyebrows wrinkled. "I don't get you."

"I don't wonder. I don't get you, either."

Blaine finished his drink and signaled the waitress for another. "Vacationing in Mexico," Blaine said, "is enough to make a rummy of anyone. It's hot and it's dry and the injunction not to drink the water is well advertised. I calculate that because Mexico's water is famous for causing diarrhea, Mexico's liquor sales are approximately three hundred percent higher than they otherwise would be."

"No one's more cynical than a good accountant," Fletch said.

"That's true," Blaine said. "Or a good reporter, I guess."

"If we're both so good," Fletch said, "how come we're both sitting here on the edge of the world, about as popular with our employers as a toothache and an earache?"

Blaine sipped his new drink. "Do I understand, from what you said before, that you've lost your job?"

"I've lost my job. I've lost my career. I couldn't get a job now even working for the *Leavenworth Levity.*"

"Is there such a newspaper?"

"Your wife's aunt said you're relentlessly literal-minded."

"Happy? You talked with Happy?"

"Of course. That's how I found you."

"My wife's aunt is sort of . . ."

". . . happy?"

"Yeah."

"She's a nice lady. Which, by Fletch definition, means she fed me."

"I'm surprised you had the resources to come find me," Blaine said. "I mean, the financial resources. The money."

"I don't," Fletch said. "Is Wagnall-Phipps paying for your so-called vacation?"

"Yes," Blaine admitted.

"I'm glad Enid Bradley didn't order you to go have your nervous breakdown on McDonald Island."

"Where's that?"

"Why don't you stop being so literal about the trivial, Mister Blaine, and become literal regarding the material."

Charles Blaine nodded his head, as if agreeing to difficult terms after a long negotiation. "All right." He sat back in his chair. "I guess I owe you an apology."

"Finally we're getting somewhere."

"I admit I was using you. Intentionally. Not

you, personally. For that, I'm sorry. I was using the press. I guess I was thinking it's okay to use the press. I didn't realize, I forgot, that the media is made up of people, flesh and blood, who can be hurt, damaged."

"Damn," said Fletch. "I forgot to bring my violin."

"That was an apology," Blaine said.

"Consider it accepted, until you hear otherwise. Now please move to the facts."

"That's what I don't know," Blaine said. "That's what I want to find out. You can hardly blame me."

"That, too, will be decided later."

"Okay, I worked—work—for Wagnall-Phipps, Inc. Not one of the world's top forty companies, but a nice, solid little concern turning over a healthy profit. Thomas Bradley, founder, creator, Chairman of the Board. A sensible man, a quiet man, a good business man. A quiet man except for the long, dirty stories he liked to tell."

"You didn't like his dirty jokes?"

"Didn't understand most of them. My wife and I lead a fairly—what should I say— conventional life. Always have." Blaine sneezed.

"I bet."

"An able business man. He'd been married to Enid for twenty years or more. Two kids."

"I've got all that."

"Rode horseback for exercise, or pleasure, or for . . . whatever reason one rides horseback."

"Good for the digestion."

"Then I began hearing he was ill."

"From whom? When?"

"Well, from Alex Corcoran, who, if you

don't know by now, is president of Wagnall-Phipps."

"I do know."

"Of course, next to Alex almost everyone looks ill. He's a big, florid man, plays golf almost every day of the week. That's all right. He makes more money for Wagnall-Phipps on the golf course than all the other sales personnel combined."

"When did Alex mention to you he thought Bradley was ill?"

"About two years ago. I don't know, really. I like to think I had noticed it myself, first."

"What did you notice?"

"About Tom? A weight loss. He seemed to be...becoming quieter. More reserved. He seemed distracted. I really don't know."

"So you understood something was wrong with him."

"Right. Then came the announcement that he was going to Europe for medical treatments. Prolonged medical treatments. Nothing was specified. When nothing is specified in a case like that, I guess, well, I guess we all thought the worst. Cancer."

"So no one, as far as you know, pressed for a full explanation."

"Of course not. It was announced that in his absence Enid Bradley would step in as Acting Chairperson."

"How come men are Chairmen and women are Chairpersons?"

"I don't know. Enid did just fine. Sometimes I'd ask her a question and she didn't have the answer, or hadn't thought it out, but by next morning she would have the answer, and it would always prove to be the correct one."

"How did you explain that to yourself? Did you think she had talked with Thomas Bradley overnight?"

"Yes, I did. At first. That made perfect sense to me, because many mornings, once or twice a week, I would get rather detailed memos from Bradley—I mean, Thomas Bradley. Nothing personal in them. Just memos regarding the backroom bookkeeping of Wagnall-Phipps."

"What do you mean, you *got them*? In the mail? From where?"

"No. They'd just be on my desk. I assumed Enid Bradley was bringing them into the office and leaving them for me."

"Okay. So the guy was in the hospital somewhere, maybe in Europe, keeping in touch with his wife by telephone, and, keeping his hand in the business by communicating with his treasurer by detailed memoranda."

"Yes. Then, last November, a Friday afternoon, the rumor went through the office that Thomas Bradley was dead. You know how rumors go through an office?"

"Ask the man who is one. A rumor, I mean."

"No one really says anything. The sound level, the tone, of an office changes. People walk differently. The expressions on their faces are different. Sometimes you just figure something is wrong, and then try to figure what is wrong. Do you know what I mean?"

"Sure. But I can't see a literal-minded man like you leaving matters like that. If there's a fact out there, somewhere, I suspect you pursue it."

"I did. I was worried, anxious. At about eight o'clock that night, I telephoned Alex Corcoran. Well, how do I say this? He had been drinking. He sounded terribly upset. He confirmed my suspicion."

"He said Thomas Bradley was dead?"

"He did. His speaking was uneven, his breathing was uneven. He said Enid was going through a terribly hard time. He asked me not to talk to Enid about it. She was being strong. She wanted no condolences, no flowers. She wasn't planning a memorial service."

"And that struck you as odd."

"Not really. The Bradleys were very quiet, sort of withdrawn people. They had few friends, if any, that I know of. The socializing they did with people in the office was perfunctory, if you know what I mean. Anyway, Alex, in a sort of drunken manner, asked me not to confront Enid with the fact of her husband's death."

"And you didn't."

"No. I was surprised to see her in the office on Monday. She didn't leave for Switzerland until Tuesday."

"Do you know she went to Switzerland?"

"Let me think. I know Alex Corcoran said she went to Switzerland."

"Because that's where Thomas Bradley died?"

"Yes. So I understood."

"How long was she gone?"

"Oh, she returned the end of the next week. Thursday or Friday."

"Ten days, roughly."

"Ten days. And all that's all right. But, like an intelligent man, like any employee, intelligent or otherwise, I wondered what effect the death would have upon the company."

"What effect did it have?"

"Zero. Except for Alex Corcoran's statement to me, it was never stated that Thomas Bradley was dead."

"You accept that."

"Only more or less. I mean, Enid's not a warm woman, but you'd think she'd plant a flower somewhere for her dead husband. She continued to be listed·as Acting Chairperson, instead of Chairperson."

"I understand that. Francine..."

"The routine remained as it was before. I mean, of course, I was expecting financial shifts in the company, little tell-tale signs, a cutting back of expenses, divestiture of certain assets, shifts of stock ownership. There was none of that. Of course the stock is held by·an instrument called The Bradley Family Company."

"You're talking about the need to pay death taxes, estate taxes, whatever they're called."

"I presumed that the family had enough personal wealth to pay taxes without touching the assets of the firm."

"Is that likely?"

"It's possible. The Bradleys have never been big spenders. As far as I know, as a family they own one house, four cars, and a horse. How much does it cost to feed a horse? The only other family expense I know of is tuition for the son."

"Might as well be poured down the drain."

"Why do you say that?"

"So everything, so far, Mister Blaine, is understandable."

"Not at all. I said the routine remained identical. In conference with Enid Bradley, clearly she would not know the answers, what to do, how to decide. The next day, she would indeed have the answer for me, and, again, it would prove to be the correct answer."

"And she wasn't talking to her husband by telephone."

"Not unless the telephone company has made a technological advance they haven't publicized." Charles Blaine's paunch trembled with his own humor.

"Do you know about Thomas Bradley's sister, Francine?"

"Yes. I understand she and Tom were very close. That she is very clever in business. That Tom frequently consulted her."

"So Enid could have been getting advice from Francine on how to run the company."

"Yes. I suppose so."

"Do you know that Enid may be only filling in for Francine? That Francine might come out to take over Wagnall-Phipps?"

Charles Blaine smiled. "It seems to me you know more about this company than you did last week when we talked, Fletcher."

"I'm doing this week what I guess I should have done two weeks ago. But, frankly, I still don't think a twelve graf story about a piddly little company like Wagnall-Phipps is worth the effort."

"So why are you doing it?"

"I'm worth the effort. I'm a good reporter."

Blaine shoved his glasses back up his sweat-slippery nose. "Yes, I know about Francine. And, yes, I think your conjecture that Enid was consulting with her is legitimate. Reasonable. Sensible."

"Thank you."

"But that doesn't explain the memos."

"Now we come to the memos."

"The memos kept coming. At first, I simply assumed they were in the pipe line—late in coming to me."

"Another reasonable assumption."

"Until they began referring to matters in the company which took place after Thomas Bradley's death."

"After."

"I said, *after,* damnit, *after.*"

"Spooky."

"Sufficient to make one wonder."

"I should think so."

"Initialed, of course. Not signed. Anyone can imitate initials. You saw the memos. You saw the initials."

"Yes. I did. That's rather the point. You showed them to me."

"Can you blame me being curious? Not only were they initialed, as always, the style of writing never varied. Not that I'm any expert on that. Purposely I showed you memos from before I heard about Bradley's death and after. Did you notice any difference?"

"I was not warned to look for any difference, thank you."

"I was curious."

"As well you might be. Did you ask anyone about these memos?"

"Yes, I mentioned the matter to Alex Corcoran. He didn't seem to understand a word I was saying. He's never understood me. I think I don't speak loudly enough for him, or something."

"He must have had some reaction. You showed him the memos, didn't you?"

"He scarcely glanced at them. He didn't understand what I was saying. He didn't listen. I went to him twice, trying to get him to see what I meant. Finally, he said, *For cryin' out loud, leave Enid alone, will you?*"

"And did you?"

"I'm an employee, Mister Fletcher."

"Okay, Mister Blaine. What was your best guess, at that point? Unless, of course, you believe that certain people have memo privileges from the beyond."

"I don't like to guess. I like to know."

"You lived with this spooky situation for some months."

"A few months."

"What were you thinking?"

"Obviously, I thought that either Enid Bradley had been writing the memos all along, and signing her husband's initials, you know, to give them added weight, authority, or.." Blaine shrugged.

"I'm filled with breathless anticipation."

"...or the memos had been being written all along by his sister, Francine, who was forging his initials, or..."

"Two oars row a boat."

"...or Thomas Bradley was not dead."

"Three oars row us in a circle."

"What do you mean?"

"You could have been forging the initials yourself."

"Why would I do that?"

"Because you're crazy."

"I suppose from your point of view there's that possibility."

"What was your best guess?"

"You're missing another possibility, Mister Fletcher. One that worried me very much. I don't know if you can understand this. I consider myself a responsible businessman. I'm a Certified Public Accountant. This other possibility kept me awake nights."

"Which was?"

"That a complete unknown was running the company, through Enid Bradley. Some completely irresponsible person, who had no true authority. Enid wouldn't be the first widow to fall into the clutches of an unscrupulous parvenu, sooth-sayer, gigolo with ambitions, what have you."

"Did the memos sound that way? Were they ignorant, irresponsible?"

"No. But some confidence men are awfully bright, or, so I understand. A sooth-sayer, or whatever you call 'em, can be right nine times out of ten. It's the tenth order you obey that puts everything into a cocked hat."

"Well, Mister Blaine, that's a possibility that I never considered."

"Well, I did. And it worried me. You've referred to me several times in this conversation as literal minded. What I am, is honest. Something funny is going on here, clearly, and I had to find out what."

"So along comes the reporter from the *News-Tribune*—"

"And, in honesty, I showed you the true instruments that are running the company of Wagnall-Phipps."

"Memos from a dead man."

"Yes."

"However, you weren't honest enough to identify them to me as such. You didn't tell me Bradley is dead."

"I've apologized for that."

" 'Oops,' said the hangman, after he dropped the hatch."

"I never realized you'd get fired. I admit to using you. I was trying to bring this matter out into the open. Clear this matter up. I have my responsibilities. Who the hell is running Wagnall-Phipps?"

"Mister Blaine, who benefits from the death of Thomas Bradley?"

"I don't know. I don't see that anyone would. The stock in Wagnall-Phipps is held in a family fund sort-of-thing, the exact nature of which I don't know. And I don't know about any personal insurance Bradley had. And I don't know who might benefit emotionally from his death."

"Interesting point that: emotionally."

"Are you suggesting he may have been murdered?"

"Mister Blaine, I have a surprise for you. Are you ready for a surprise?"

"I'd love some answers."

"This isn't an answer. It's just a surprise."

"What is it?"

"Thomas Bradley did not die in Switzerland. I checked."

Charles Blaine stared at Fletch a long moment. "That's more of a question than an answer, isn't it?"

"Precisely."

Blaine leaned forward, his elbows on the table. "To answer your question more specifically: financially, I suspect the chief beneficiary of Thomas Bradley's death would be The Internal Revenue Service."

"And you said you can see no signs of estate taxes being paid."

"Exactly. Which is another worry. I do not intend to be party to a tax fraud. I do not even want to look like I might have been party to a tax fraud."

"Right," said Fletch. "Better my career be ruined than yours."

Sweating, his face colored, Blaine sat back. "I'm sorry it looks that way to you. It must. I did a very wrong thing."

"Tut tut, think nothing of it. Petroleum on a duck's feathers."

Blaine looked at his empty glass. "I don't get that expression. What happens when you put petroleum on a duck's feathers?"

"The duck drowns."

"Oh." Blaine cast his eyes slowly over the beach, which was empty at noon time. "We don't seem to know any more than we did when we started, do we?"

"Has Enid Bradley ever explicitly stated to you that her husband is dead?"

"Yes. Last Thursday. After your newspaper report came out. Just before she said I must be crazy and insisted Mary and I take a nice long vacation to this Mexican paradise." Blaine sneezed and then laughed.

"Was it Enid Bradley who specified Puerto de San Orlando?"

"Yes. She's paying."

"But you've been to Mexico before."

Blaine sneezed again. "Acapulco."

"I see."

"Dusty place, this. When are you going back?"

"Can't get a plane until tomorrow noon."

"What are you going to do until then?"

"Snooze on the beach, I guess."

"Will you permit Mary and me to entertain you at dinner tonight?"

"Certainly," Fletch said. "Nice of you."

"Not really," said Blaine. "Seems to me, without really meaning to, I did you a lot of harm." He stood up. "Will nine o'clock be all right?"

"See you then," Fletch said.

"The hotel's terrace diningroom." Blaine put out his hand to shake. "Why don't we stop this 'Mister Blaine, Mister Fletcher' nonsense? I suspect we're both victims of the same accident—or, I got you into my accident, or something."

Fletch stood and shook hands. "Okay, Charley."

"Do I call you Irwin?"

"Not if you want to live till dinner. I answer to the name Fletch."

Blaine leaned toward Fletch, his eyes magnified through his glasses. "Fletch, am I crazy, or is the world crazy?"

"That," said Fletch, "seems an eminently sane question."

26

Three people, Mary Blaine, Charles Blaine, and Fletch, at dinner under the stars on the hotel terrace in Puerto de San Orlando, Mexico.

Charles: Gin and tonics, please, with lime.

Fletch (to Mary Blaine): I've met your Aunt. She's a real nice lady. She fed me.
Mary: Isn't she marvelous? She says she was born happy, and I believe it. That woman has had such suffering, such tragedy. Yet she is relentlessly happy.
Fletch: I know her nickname is Happy. What's her real name?
Mary: Mabel.

Mary: Look at the moon.

Charles: Even in Puerto de San Orlando I suspect prices are a little higher per item than they need be. I know it's a new resort, or a resort-to-be, and the Mexican government is trying to attract people here. But I daresay, if you drive a few miles inland, into some of the real villages, you'll find everything from limes to curios at half the prices...

Charles: Gin and tonics, please. With lime.

Mary: There's something unreal about Enid Bradley. I mean, she's the only contemporary woman I know who seems to have been born in a corset.

Fletch: Originally, Tom Bradley was from Dallas, Texas?
Mary: You mean from where men are men?
Charles: I don't know.

Mary: Enid always looks terrified of what the next moment will bring—you know, as if she's afraid someone is going to say something dirty.
Charles: Her husband usually does. I mean, did.

Charles: Gin and tonics. Lime.

Mary: Look at the moons.
Charles: Didn't I say something this morning, Fletch, about people vacationing in Mexico drinking three times more alcohol than usual? They make a lot of money off our fear of drinking the local water.

Mary: I mean, I just don't see anyone ever having a rollicking time in bed with Enid Bradley, ever. I mean, I just can't picture Enid Bradley without her sensible shoes on.

Mary: Isn't this romantic, Charley? Look at the moons in the ocean. I have an idea. Why don't we take this nice boy to bed?

Charlie: Mary, I think we should order dinner, don't you?

Fletch: Is Thomas Bradley dead?
Mary: Why wouldn't he be?
Charles: Frankly, I don't think so. I think he committed some gross irregularity and decided to disappear. Trouble is, I can't find what gross irregularity he committed. As Treasurer of Wagnall-Phipps, it's my damned responsibility to find it. I'm a Certified Public Accountant, and I can't find anything wrong. Please forgive me, Fletch. Please understand. This is very worrisome to me.
Mary: He's dead. It's just that nobody cares much.

27

Upon his return to his apartment late Wednesday night, Fletch found on the coffee table, beside the bills and junk mail, a note and three letters of interest.

F—
Your X, Linda, called. I told her you're cruising off Mexico on your yacht.

—M.

Dear Mister Fletcher:
The Mayor has informed his office that he has decided to honor you with the Good Citizen of The Month Award in recognition of the heroic risking your own life to save the life of another citizen on the Guilden Street Bridge Sunday night.
The ceremony is to take place in the Mayor's office Friday at ten o'clock sharp.

You are to report to Mrs. Goldovsky at The Mayor's Office, City Hall, at eight-thirty sharp Friday morning. Mrs. Goldovsky will instruct you in what you are to do and to say during and after the ceremony. Any tardiness in meeting with Mrs. Goldovsky will not be tolerated.

The ceremony will be by nature of a press conference, which is to say, members of the press— reporters, photographers, and cameramen will be in attendance. Your being dressed in normal business attire will be suitable.

Sincerely,

The Office of The Mayor

Dear Mister Fletcher—

I read about how you rescued that lady off the bridge? I need rescuing. My parents treat me awful bad. They're never taken me to FANTAZYLAND— not even oncet, in all my life. Please come quick and rescue me up.

Tommy address above

Dear Mister Fletcher:

Although I'm sure I join millions in praising your act of heroism Sunday night, in saving that expectant woman from suicide, perhaps only my associate, Mister Smith, of this hotel, and I know you to be not an entirely honest man. There was a report of your deed in this morning's Chronicle. *We were able to recognize from your picture the man who was in my office last Thursday, identifying himself as Geoffrey Armistad. You showed us a wallet you said you found somewhere off the hotel's property containing twenty five thousand dollars cash, apparently belonging to a recent guest of this hotel, a Mister James St. E. Crandall. Such were the names we gave to the police, in reporting this incident. You gave us every assurance you, too, would report to the police. Apparently, you did no such thing. In fact, the newspaper reports you resigned your job with the News-Tribune last Friday. (You stated to us you were employed as a parking-lot attendant.) All this indicates to us you have no intention of returning the money to its rightful owner. Mister Smith and I think it only fair to warn you that we have set matters right this end, and provided the police with your correct name, and, having spent two minutes with the telephone directory, your correct address. Doubtlessly they will be in touch with you, requiring you to turn the money over to them until proper disposition can be made.*

Yours, Sincerely,

Jacques Cavalier,
Manager
Park Worth Hotel

28

"Where's the thousand dollars?"

"Hell of a way to greet me." At nearly midnight Moxie stood in the doorway of the apartment and dropped her airline's bag onto the floor. The zipper of the bag was broken and sticking out of it were the playscript, a sneaker, and a towel.

"Hello," Fletch said from the divan.

"Hello."

"You look bushed."

"I am bushed. Been rehearsing since noon. You look bushed with a sunburn. Oh, no! You have a sunburn!"

Through the dim light of the livingroom she was looking at him like a cosmetician.

"I have a sunburn. I fell asleep on the beach."

"Do you have it all over?"

"All over what?"

"All over your bod."

"No. Thank you for asking."

"That's all right. I guess it will fade before opening night. You'll just look funny tomorrow, that's all. At rehearsal."

"I'm not going to rehearsal tomorrow."

"Fletch, you have to."

"I do?"

"Sam is just impossible in the role. His manners are just so heavy. He's so self-conscious."

"And don't forget he's cursed with thick thighs or something."

"You'd think he was playing *Streetcar Named Desire*. His timing is all off for comedy. I told Paul you'd absolutely be at the rehearsal tomorrow."

"Paul the director?"

"Paul the director. He's good to give you the chance, seeing you've never really acted before. I mean, in the theater."

"I will not be at the theater tomorrow absolutely. Or tomorrow or tomorrow or tomorrow. Isn't that a line from somewhere?"

"Almost. I told you you can act."

"I've already done the strip-tease once today. And that was without music."

Moxie was taking things out of her airline's bag and spreading them around the floor. "Tell me: you were kidnapped and raped by a gang of Mexican Girl Scouts—right?"

"Almost. Customs. Coming back. The United States Customs. They hustled me into a little room, made me strip, and proceeded to prod and poke in my every crevasse and orifice."

"Serious?"

"I thought it was serious. I didn't like it much. They X-rayed my boots, my suitcase, my teeth."

"That's terrible."

"They spent over two hours on me. Or in me."

"What for?"

"They were unwilling to believe anyone my age flew on three airplanes to Puerto de San Orlando, Mexico, and back on three airplanes for thirty hours on the beach. I told them I had some time off."

"They thought you were smuggling drugs or something."

"Something." Fletch flicked a finger at the letter from the Mayor's Office on the coffee table. "Hardly the way to treat the Good Citizen of the Month."

Moxie knelt on the divan next to him and took Fletch's head in her arms. "Aw, my poor Fletch. Were you able to fart on cue?"

"Of course it didn't help convince them of my innocence that I was carrying over one thousand dollars in cash in my pocket."

"Did they finally apologize to the Good Citizen?"

"They said they'd catch me next time. Now may I ask where the thousand dollars is?"

"What thousand dollars?"

"The thousand dollars you took from the wallet."

"Oh, that thousand dollars."

"The very same."

"I bought a sweater."

"A thousand dollar sweater?"

"A skirt. Some records. And some baloney. Want a baloney sandwich?"

"We're living higher on the hog."

"And a car."

"A car!"

"A little car. Even smaller than yours."

"What kind of a car?"

"Yellow."

"A *yellow* car. I see."

"And it does beep-beep nicely."

"A small yellow car with a horn. Have I got it right so far?"

"I suppose it has an engine. It has an ignition key, which works."

"What a relief. No one should look at the engine until the ignition key doesn't work. Might be bad luck."

"I needed a car. You know, to get around."

"So the thousand dollars is gone."

"No such thing! I have a skirt, a sweater, some records—some nice records—a car, and some baloney. That's not *gone*, like, you know, if I threw it out the window. Want a baloney sandwich?"

"Sure."

At the kitchen counter Moxie spread the mustard so thin the baloney didn't even look slippery.

"Are you trying to make it last until all men are free?" he asked.

"What?"

"The mustard." He took the jar and knife from her and slathered it on properly.

Sitting at the kitchen table, she asked, "What were you doing in Mexico? I mean, other than smuggling diamonds and drugs and cruising in your yacht?"

"I went to see Charles Blaine, Vice-president and treasurer of Wagnall-Phipps."

"Oh."

"And he tells me," Fletch said, placing the top pieces of bread on the sandwiches carefully so they would not slip, "that he's been receiving memos from a dead man."

"Seems I read that in the newspaper. Sort of."

"Indirectly, I suppose you did."

"So what's new?"

"Obviously, he has not been receiving memos from a dead man."

"It's nice to hear you say that. For a while, you had me worried."

"So from whom has he been receiving memos?"

"Must be Madame Palonka."

"Must be." He handed her a sandwich. "Who's Madame Palonka?"

"A medium in San Francisco. She transmits messages from the dead. Wow. Too much mustard."

"Who has been continuing to write memos signed Thomas Bradley after Thomas Bradley died?"

"A secretary stuck on routine?"

"Who is running Wagnall-Phipps?"

"Who cares?"

"I think they thought no one would care—much."

"They're right. Who are 'they'?"

"The great 'they'. I dunno."

"You care."

"I either have to care, or consider myself a non-entity, you see."

"Phew! What a choice! To be a something or not to be a nothing...how does that work out? To be a something, or a something...? God! I can't keep up with you."

"Something's rotten in Denmark. Is that the same play?"

"Nothing's rotten in Denmark," Moxie said. "I've been there. Surely no one in Denmark would give me a mustard sandwich which even the baloney is trying to slip away from."

"Charles Blaine cares who's running Wagnall-Phipps."

"Fletch, do you think—just possibly—you're slightly obsessed with this matter?"

"It's not often one sees memos from a dead man."

"I admit that."

"And it's not often, I hope, that one's career is ruined by the self-same mysterious memos."

"So you insist that your compulsion to find out who wrote those memos and why is legitimate?"

"I insist."

"Why don't you forget this whole silly thing, come to rehearsals tomorrow, try out for the lead in *In Love,* work hard with me, and enjoy a smashing success? You might find a whole new career for yourself in the theater."

"Sure. And ever after I'd still be known as the journalist who got fired because I quoted a dead man."

"At least come to rehearsal tomorrow."

"Can't."

"Why not?"

"Going to New York."

"Going to New York? You can't!"

"Can too. Made my reservation on an early flight while I was waiting for you."

"Why are you going to New York?"

"Because there's still one person concerned with this whole matter I haven't yet seen—Tom Bradley's sister, Francine."

"What can she know about it? She's all the way across the country!"

"Yeah. I know. But she's the only one I see benefitting from Bradley's death. Unless, of course, you subscribe to the theory Mrs. Bradley benefits emotionally by having gotten rid of the old boy."

"I don't subscribe to any theory. Except that there comes a time to give up! And you're long past that time!"

"Francine Bradley," Fletch said patiently, "is going to come West at some point and take over, run Wagnall-Phipps. Tom Bradley has been consulting her for years. Enid Bradley consults her. Don't you think I ought to at least go look in her eyes and try to figure out what all this means to her?"

"I suspect she'll look you back in the eyes and say you're a nut. All this can be explained by a secretarial mistake, Fletch."

"I don't think so. Charles Blaine doesn't think so."

"Anyhow, it was announced in this morning's *News-Trib* you're being honored Friday in the Mayor's Office for being Good Guy of The Week."

"Good Citizen of the Month, if you please."

"You can't go to New York. You have an appointment with the Mayor."

"The Mayor has an appointment with the press. I don't expect to be there."

"For goodness' sake, why not? If we could

announce by Friday you're a member of the cast of *In Love* opening soon at The Colloquial Theater—"

"Everybody's got an angle."

"You bet."

"I'll be in New York Friday. You're not eating your sandwich."

Moxie pushed her plate away from her. "Your culinary skills aren't up to baloney sandwiches, Fletch. Better stick to peanut butter sandwiches for a while yet."

29

The doorman of the expensive, tall East Side New York apartment house put his hand over the mouthpiece of his telephone and said, with mild surprise and perfect respect, "Ms. Bradley says she doesn't know you, Mister Fletcher."

Fletch held out his hand for the phone. "May I speak to her myself, please?"

"Of course, sir."

He handed the phone to Fletch and stepped back half a pace. He was young and lean and had steady eyes and the gold braid on his uniform looked as ridiculous as a spinnaker on an aircraft carrier.

"Ms. Bradley?" Fletch said into the phone.

The woman's voice was throaty. "Yes?"

"Ms. Bradley, my name is Fletcher. I need to speak to you regarding the management of your late brother's company, Wagnall-Phipps. I have come all the way from California just to do so."

After a pause, Francine Bradley asked, "Who are you, Mister Fletcher?"

"I'm a reporter—an ex-reporter—who did a story for the financial pages of the *News-Tribune* on Wagnall-Phipps. I guess I made some sort of a mistake in writing the story. Yet I still don't know what the truth is."

"How could I help you?"

"I don't know. But I've talked with your sister-in-law, Enid Bradley, your niece, Roberta, your nephew, Tom—"

"The person you should speak to is Alex Corcoran. He's the president."

"I have spoken with him. I've also spoken again—a few days ago—with Charles Blaine."

There was a long pause. "You've spoken within the last few days with Charles Blaine?"

"I went to Mexico to do so."

"Well, you certainly have gone far out of your way. Weren't Corcoran and Blaine able to help you?"

"Not much."

"I don't see how I can help you. But come up. Anyone who's gone to as much expense and trouble as you have shouldn't be turned away at the door."

"Okay," Fletch said. "I'll give you back to the doorman."

"Really, Mister Fletcher—do I have the name right?"

"Yes."

"You could have saved yourself an awful lot of

expense and bother if you'd simply called me from California. I probably could have told you on the phone whether I could help you..."

Francine Bradley had opened the door of Apartment 21M, flickered her eyes at him in some surprise, and immediately began talking as if she were continuing the conversation they had had on the apartment house's telephone.

Her hair was blonde and well set. Her face looked as if she had had expensive skin care. Her necklace was of heavy gold braid; her earrings matched. Her dress was a well-made, comfortably formal green satin, cut low in front. She was noticeably slim for a lady in her mid-forties.

"...I doubt I know as much about Tom's company as you think." She led the way into a livingroom furnished well but sparsely. Glare filled the room from the large window overlooking the city. "I know none of the personnel out there, personally. I am acquainted with the figures, of course. Since Tom's death, well, Enid has had to lean on me more than somewhat. Enid, as you probably know, had no experience in business."

Her back to the window, Francine faced Fletch, hesitated as if wondering if she had already answered all his questions. Only at his silence did she gesture toward the divan. "Well, sit down. I'm expected out for dinner, shortly, but let me help you however I can in whatever time I have."

Sitting, Fletch unbuttoned his jacket, hitched up his trouser legs to avoid wrinkling his new suit.

On the coffee table in front of him were her handbag and gloves.

"I appreciate your seeing me," Fletch said. She sat on a brightly flowered chair, her back to the light from the window. "You may think me odd before I'm done, but I hope at least you will understand my confusion."

"I'm sure I won't think you a bit odd, Mister Fletcher." She smiled as if she already thought him odd. "Although, I must admit, when you said you're a reporter, an ex-reporter, I guess I was expecting to open the door to someone...more mature, older, I mean...someone who might look like he's been through more wars than you do."

"I keep an innocent look." Fletch smiled. "It comes from mixing orange juice with my cereal."

Francine Bradley laughed happily.

Now that his eyes had adjusted to the glare in the room, Fletch saw the photographs on a bookshelf of Roberta Bradley, Thomas Bradley, Jr., school photographs of them at various ages, two photographs of Enid Bradley, a younger and an older, and a large group photograph of the family. Fletch assumed the dark-haired man with his arm around Enid's waist was Thomas Bradley. On the wall facing him, Fletch saw a brown and black tile mosaic. On a low table near the window was an unfinished mosaic.

"Did your brother do the mosaic on the wall?" Fletch asked.

"Yes." Francine looked sadly at it. Then she sighed and gestured at the unfinished mosaic on the low table. "And that's one he was working on. Tom used to stay with me, you know, when he was in New York to see the doctors. He was working on that just before he went off to Switzerland. I've left it there. Silly of me, I suppose. It just makes him seem—well—sometimes when I come in at night I almost feel I can see him sitting there, in his robe and slippers, working on it."

"I guess my questions will seem strange to you."

"That's all right." She glanced at her watch. "I am being picked up..."

"Yes. I guess the point of my questions is that when I went to do a report on Wagnall-Phipps I was shown recent memos from your brother, and quoted from them. As a result, of course, I was fired."

At first she looked at him as if he were speaking a language she didn't understand. "What do you mean, 'recent'?"

"Dated as recently as a few weeks ago."

"Tom died a year ago."

"That's why I'm here."

Francine looked at her red-polished finger nails in her lap. "What an odd thing."

"Yes. It is odd."

"What's the explanation?"

"I wish I knew."

"Who showed you these memos?"

"Charles Blaine. Vice-president and treasurer of Wagnall-Phipps. Generally, one would think, a reliable source."

"Oh, Blaine. They've had trouble with him before. Enid has mentioned it. I think he might be very good at what he does, but... Enid says he takes everything so seriously. Sort of an ogre to his own department." Francine nodded her head. "Yes, I can see that, from what I've heard of Blaine. If every T isn't crossed, every I dotted apparently he has conniptions."

"This isn't a case of T's not crossed and I's not

dotted, Ms. Bradley. This is a case of memos which were initialed—by someone who wasn't alive to initial them."

Francine shrugged. "Then someone's playing a bad joke. Someone in the secretarial pool. One of the people working with Blaine. I can see where someone working under a tight man like Blaine might want to play a game on him, shake him up, confront him with something inexplicable."

"It could be."

"What did Enid say, when you asked her?"

"She thinks Blaine is having a nervous breakdown. She sent him to Mexico for a vacation."

"Then that is probably so."

"I went to Mexico. He doesn't seem to be having a nervous breakdown. He seems to be having a hot, dusty time."

"Are you qualified to judge, Mister Fletcher? Have you a degree in psychiatry?"

"I left it in my other suit."

"I don't mean to sound like a prosecuting attorney. It's just that . . . most people can put on a good face. There's always more going on under people's surfaces than we'd suspect."

"Charles Blaine assures me he did not forge those memos."

Again Francine shrugged. "Then someone's playing a nasty trick on him." She smiled at Fletch pleasantly. "The Halloween spirit still walks the earth. People in offices love to play games on each other."

"Ms. Bradley, when precisely did your brother die?"

"I've already said—a year ago."

"Enid says the same thing. Yet Corcoran and Blaine both say he died six months later—last November."

"Oh, that. I don't blame you for being confused by that. Tom did die a year ago. We weren't prepared for it. Enid had been put in as Acting Chairperson of Wagnall-Phipps in Tom's absence, and she had hardly gotten her feet wet. I think people tolerated her in the job because they knew Tom was coming back. She was backed by Tom's authority, you see. She talked to me about it. We decided to, let's say, delay the news of Tom's death until she was more firmly established as Chairperson. Can you understand that?"

"Yes. I suppose."

"There was another consideration. A more human reason. Enid was terribly in love with my brother. From all I know, people working for Wagnall-Phipps—people like Corcoran and Blaine, others—were terrifically fond of him. Enid wanted to mourn alone a while. Trying to run the company—well, she just couldn't take the long faces, the commiseration, of the people upon whom she had to depend. Do you see?"

Fletch wrinkled his brow.

"There were lots of reasons for delaying the news of the death. The younger staff would have deserted the company, at least until they had more confidence in Enid . . . lots of reasons."

"Your brother died a year ago. The news wasn't given the people at Wagnall-Phipps until six months later, on a Friday afternoon in November. And it wasn't until the following Tuesday that Enid left for Switzerland. Is that right?"

Francine's eyes ran over the mosaic on the

wall as if she were trying to remember. "Yes. That's about right." Her eyes then met his. "You're asking why we didn't go to Switzerland immediately, six months earlier, at the news of Tom's death?"

"That's the question."

"It was our decision of the moment. Tom was dead. We'd had no warning of it. The news didn't reach Enid until twenty four hours after the death. A cremation was recommended. Enid cabled permission. It wasn't until six months later that we went to Switzerland, had a memorial service, for just the two of us, brought home Tom's ashes."

"You went to Switzerland with Enid?"

"Didn't I just say so?"

"Where in Switzerland?"

"Tom died in a small clinic outside Geneva."

Fletch took a deep breath and shook his head. "Ms. Bradley, your brother didn't die in Switzerland."

Looking at him, her eyebrows shot up. "Now what are you saying?"

Tiredly, Fletch said, "I've checked with the American Embassy in Switzerland. No American citizen named Thomas Bradley has died in Switzerland last year, or at any time in recent history."

Her lips a perfect little O, Francine sucked in breath. "They said that?"

"So said the American Embassy in Geneva."

"That's not possible, Mister Fletcher."

"And I'm sure they're not playing a prank."

"Well." And Francine opened and closed her mouth silently. "I don't know what to say."

"Neither do I."

"I guess we'll just have to chalk it up to a bureaucratic mistake. I'll have someone look into it."

"This information came with the assurance from the Embassy that regarding in-country deaths, their records are one hundred percent accurate."

"Oh, Mister Fletcher. If you can ever show me any bureaucracy of any country being one hundred percent accurate about anything I'll jump over the moon in a single leap."

Fletch sat forward in the divan. "You see, Ms. Bradley, I have many questions, about many things."

There was a buzzing from the foyer.

"Excuse me," she said. She went into the foyer and there was the sound of a phone being picked up and Francine Bradley said, "Hello? . . . yes. Please tell Mister Savenor I'll be down in five minutes."

When Francine Bradley returned to the livingroom, Fletch was standing near the window. He said, referring to the unfinished mosaic on the low table, "You've even left the loose tiles out."

"Yes," she said. "They're pretty in themselves."

"May we meet again?" he asked.

"Yes. I'm sure you mean to be helpful."

"I suspect I've surprised you enough for the moment, anyway."

"I'm sure there's a reasonable explanation for everything," Francine Bradley said. "A nasty office prank . . . a death certificate misfiled at the Embassy."

"Probably."

"Are you free for dinner tomorrow night?"

"That would be nice. Where, when?"

"Do you like French cuisine?"

"I like food."

"Why don't you meet me at eight o'clock at Chez Claire? It's only two blocks from here." She pointed more or less south.

"Eight o'clock," he said.

She followed him into the foyer. "I'm sorry I have to go now," she said. "I'm curious about what more you have to say." She held the door open for him. "I'm sure we can figure all this out," she said. "Together."

Beside the doorman, there was only one man waiting in the lobby. He was a silver-haired man in his fifties in a pearl gray suit seeming to look comfortable in an impossibly stiff-looking, narrow-seated, high-backed chair.

30

Friday morning at quarter to eight, Fletch stood in the drizzle across the street from Francine Bradley's East Side apartment house. He had bought a raincoat and a rainhat and, the night before, in Times Square, a pair of clear eyeglasses, and he was wearing all this, and under one arm he carried a copy of *The New York Post*. He supposed he looked like someone not wanting to be noticed.

He was waiting for Francine Bradley to come out of the apartment building, but to his surprise, at ten minutes past eight a taxi stopped in front of the building and Francine Bradley got out of the cab and dashed into the building. She was wearing a short rain coat and high boots.

At nine twenty she came out of the building dressed in a longer raincoat and apparently a suit or skirt and began hailing cabs. The doorman was blowing his whistle for her.

On his side of the street, Fletch got a cab more quickly.

Getting into the taxi, Fletch said, "U-turn and stop, please."

The driver did so.

Fletch said, "See that woman trying to get a taxi?"

"Yeah."

"I want to see where she's going."

The driver looked at him through the rearview mirror. "You some kind of a pervert?"

Fletch said, "Internal Revenue Service."

The driver said, "Bastard. Better you should be a pervert."

They followed Francine's cab downtown where it stopped in front of the Bennett Bank Building.

"See?" Fletch said. "The lady's leading me to her money."

"I wish I could charge you more." The driver leaned over to read his meter. "I got to pay taxes, too, you know. Do you guys from Internal Revenue Service tip?"

"Yeah," said Fletch. "And we report the person to whom we give the tip—name, date, and place—just to see if you report it."

The driver turned around in his seat. "I don't want your damned tip! Get out of my cab!"

"Okay," Fletch said.

"Jeez!" the driver slapped the change into Fletch's hand. "Government in front of me in blue uniforms...government in my back seat!"

"Sure you don't have change of a dime?"

"Get outta my cab!"

Fletch waited a few minutes before entering the Bennet Bank Building.

On the sign board in the lobby was listed *Bradley & Co.—Investments.*

He returned to the bank building at noon and followed Francine Bradley to Wayne's Steak House. She was accompanied by a man not much more than twenty carrying a brief case. His suit was not particularly good, his shoes were dull, he was without a raincoat, but his brief case was new-looking. They were in the restaurant fifty minutes. Fletch followed them back to the building and loitered in the lobby an hour. During that time the young man did not leave the building.

Fletch returned to the Bennet Bank Building again just before five o'clock. At five ten Francine Bradley came out and took a taxi. At five twenty-five, the young man came out and began walking down the street.

Fletch followed him into the subway, onto the platform and, while ostensibly waiting for a train, drew attention to himself by staring at the young man. Eventually the young man gave Fletch a look of distaste, and it was then that Fletch approached him.

"Sorry," Fletch said. "Trying to figure it out. Didn't I see you at lunch today at Wayne's Steak House with Francine?"

The young man's facial expression cleared. "You know Ms. Bradley?"

"Sure," Fletch said. "I've consulted her about some of my investments. Brilliant lady."

"She is." The young man nodded emphatically. "I think I'm damned lucky to be working for her. An education."

"She handles her brother's money, doesn't she? It was Tom who sent me to her."

"Well, we handle the Bradley Family Company. Mostly Wagnall-Phipps, you know. Other stuff. Not much I mean, not millions. But she's damned clever with what there is."

"Why doesn't Tom handle it himself?"

The young man looked surprised at Fletch, hesitated, then said, "Didn't you know? Her brother died. A year ago."

"Gee, I didn't know. Too bad. Guess it's been a while since I've seen good ol' Tom. How long you been working with Francine?"

"Seven months." A train was coming in. "Real education."

The young man waited for Fletch to board the train first.

"Not my train," Fletch said.

"This is the only train you can get from here," the young man said.

"I'll wait for a less crowded train," Fletch said before noticing the train wasn't crowded at all.

As the train pulled off, the young man stared at Fletch through the window. On his face, expressionlessness battled curiosity, and lost.

At eight o'clock, Fletch entered Chez Claire and found Francine Bradley waiting for him, already seated at a table for two against the back wall.

There was a candle on the table.

31

"I think your nephew, Tom, is in serious trouble," Fletch said. They had ordered vodka gimlets on the rocks. "I saw him last Sunday."

Over the candle, he checked Francine's facial expression and saw that it conveyed the proper concern. More than proper—genuine. Francine Bradley did not strike Fletch as simply the distant maiden aunt going through kind, formal motions toward her late brother's family. Still, he realized, there had to be limits to her knowledge and her involvement with the family.

"What do you mean?" she asked, her tone near fear. "I understand Tom is in pre-med and doing very well."

"Not quite. He's using whatever education he has in chemistry to swallow oblivion."

"Drugs? Tom's on drugs?"

Fletch said, "Seems a mess. Hasn't attended

classes since last fall. His roommate has him ensconced in a cushioned bathtub where he dreams away his days and nights. Doesn't know what else to do with him."

"Oh, no! Not Tom."

"I promised I would try to do what I could for him—which is another reason I'm seeing you. Of course, he makes no sense at all about his father's death."

"What does he say about Tom's death?"

"He sort of says your brother killed himself. He sort of blames your brother for dying. Sort of common, I believe, for a young person to be angry at a parent for dying, for leaving him. Sometimes young people blame themselves for a parent's death."

"You're playing psychiatrist again, Mister Fletcher."

"I'm called Fletch," Fletch said. "And I'm not playing psychiatrist. I'm in a crazy situation—and so are you—and I'm trying to understand it."

"I'm not in any situation at all."

"You are, too," Fletch said. "The preponderance of funds you're investing through your little company in the Bennet Bank Building came from your brother." Instantly, her eyes narrowed. "I'm checking to find out what probate action has been taken on your brother's estate—I suspect, none has. There's a pretty good suspicion that you and Enid are simply avoiding taxes. It's been stated to me by none other than Enid Bradley that you intend to go to California and take over the running of Wagnall-Phipps yourself. Anyone who didn't guess you've been forging your brother's initials to those accounting memos the last year would have to be myopic."

The waiter laid their gimlets before them. As in most dimly lit restaurants Fletch had experienced, the waiter's hands were dirty.

"You seem to be upset, Fletch." Francine sipped her drink. "Will you call me Francine?"

"With pleasure."

"Per usual with you," Francine said, "I don't really know what to say. You come in from California with all this information, all these questions ...I am most upset by what you just said about Tom."

"He needs help. Heavy help. Quicker than soonest."

"I just had no idea..."

"Apparently he can fool his mother. He gets cleaned up, goes home, says he's doing well in school, gets money, then settles back in his bathtub with a six pack of downers."

In the candlelight, tears glistened in Francine's eyes. "I assure you," she said, "something will be done about it—immediately. Quicker than soonest. I appreciate your telling me."

"In a way," Fletch said, "Ta-ta, your niece, worries me just as much. Tom's roommate refers to her as a wind-up toy. She seems to be straight-arming existence, protecting herself in a girls' school, protecting Tom. I know their father died—a year ago—but they both seem inordinately troubled."

"When I get out there..." Francine said. "There's only so much Enid can handle."

"When are you going?"

"I'm afraid it will be another few months. I still have things to wind up here."

"You are going to run Wagnall-Phipps?"

"Tom wanted me to. Enid wants me to. I sold my business—a small business—a few years ago."

Fletch considered his gimlet, sipped it, looked across the flame at her. "Do you have any answers to the questions I just asked?"

"You mean, are Enid and I perpetrating a tax fraud?"

"Yeah, for starters."

"Not as far as I know. Of course, it's entirely possible Enid hasn't done things exactly right. In fact I'd say it's highly likely. She's not a Charles Blaine. She hasn't any training, any experience, except for having lived with Tom. I would expect she's screwed up mightily, but I'm sure with no intention to defraud."

"Have you been forging those memos?" Fletch asked easily.

"I've been consulting with my sister-in-law by telephone. Almost daily. Seeing you're so good at doing your homework—knowing about my office in the Bennet Bank Building and what I do there—you might check our telephone bills. Enid's and mine. They're monumental."

"Then we're still without explanations."

"Why don't we fortify ourselves with another drink, a good dinner, then go back to my apartment? We can talk more there. I suppose no one's ever told you that you're attractive?"

"Only a United States Customs Officer."

She put her hand on his. "Don't worry. I'm not one of these middle-aged women eager to get into the trousers of young men. Your orange juice-and-cereal innocence will remain intact with me." She took her hand away and picked up the menu. "They serve a very good orange duck here."

"Let's go over this one more time," Fletch said.

It was eleven fifteen when they entered Francine's apartment. They had had three cocktails, four courses, shared two bottles of wine and finished up with brandy for him, crème de menthe for her. During most of the entree Francine had told a long, wandering story which had ended with a punchline more barnyard than funny.

At the apartment, Fletch dropped his coat on the divan and then himself. He loosened his shirt collar, and, slumped, put his head on the back rest.

Quietly, she said, "Anything you say."

The lights were subdued. Francine Bradley was moving noiselessly around the room. The sounds of violins began coming from the walls.

"I'll just put on the coffee."

He concentrated on the violins. Their breathing was reminiscent of a full-bosomed girl whose passion had been awaken. He heard the rustle of Francine's dress as she entered the room.

Softly, her voice asked, "Now what are your questions?" She was sitting, relaxed, in the flowered chair.

"Who told you your brother was dead?"

"Enid. She called me at the office. She was terribly upset. Crying. Incoherent. I called her back an hour later. In fact, we talked most of the night."

"And you both decided not to go to Switzerland immediately?"

"Actually, we decided that the next morning. When the news first came, we weren't of any mind to decide anything. By the next morning, when we had both had some rest, Tom had already been dead two days. It would take us another two days to get to Switzerland, what with Enid being in California, and I being in New York, and each of us working. Instead, Enid cabled permission for the cremation."

"Okay. And then business went on as usual, you counseling Enid daily by phone."

"Yes."

"Then, in November, you both went to Switzerland?"

"Yes."

"Together?"

"Yes. Enid stopped over here, a night and a day. We flew over together."

"What did you do when you got there?"

"Rented a car. Checked into a hotel. Rested. Next day, Enid collected the ashes from the mortuary. It took time for us to arrange a little prayer service, in a chapel. We knew no one. In fact, we did not apply to the Embassy for help—we didn't think of it. We did have a service, late in the afternoon, Tuesday, I think, in a little chapel not far from the clinic. Just Enid, myself, and the minister. He spoke English. Enid brought the ashes to the service, and the minister had them on a little table, on an altar, throughout."

"Then you and Enid returned together to New York with the ashes."

The water pot in the kitchen was whistling.

"Yes," Francine said. "Enid flew on to California."

"How come the kids didn't go to Switzerland with you?"

"Tom and Ta-ta?"

"Yes."

"At that point, Enid thought they were just beginning to get over the death. She didn't want to stir up their grief all over again. Remember, this was six months later." Francine stood up. "Let me get the coffee."

When she returned to the livingroom, Fletch was sitting up, his elbows on his knees. In her absence he had paced up and down the livingroom. On the low table near the window the mosaic was more nearly finished than he remembered. He looked out the window at the roofs and lights of other buildings before returning to the divan. She placed a cup of coffee in front of him and took her own cup to her chair.

"Francine," Fletch said, stirring his coffee. "I think your sister-in-law murdered your brother."

Her cup jumped in her saucer. "God!" she said. "Now what are you saying?"

"I think your dear, incompetent sister-in-law cleverly has walked you through a complete illusion—which you have believed."

Francine's breathing was suddenly shallow, her jaw muscles tight. She swallowed twice, rapidly. "Really, Fletch! You are putting me through an awful lot!"

"Sorry," he said. "I'm afraid I have some evidence."

"Of murder?" Her voice was almost a shriek.

"Of murder," he said softly. "I haven't been

confronting you with this evidence until I knew you, a little bit, and, well, until I was sure..."

"Sure of the evidence, or sure I can take it?"

"Oh, I'm sure of the evidence."

"All right, Fletcher." Francine Bradley was sitting straight and stiff in her chair, staring white-faced through the dim light at Fletch. "What's your evidence?"

"Ashes, represented to be your brother's, are not."

"Ashes..." She seemed to be trying to repeat what he had just said. "Not my brother's ashes?"

"No. They are not your brother's ashes."

"How can anyone tell a thing like that?"

"Last Saturday night—early Sunday morning—I went to Enid's house in Southworth and took a small sample of the ashes from the urn. The previous afternoon, Enid had showed them to me and said they were your brother's ashes."

"You broke into my brother's house?"

"The door was unlocked. I had the ashes analysed."

"You stole my brother's ashes?" Her throat muscles were so constricted her voice was barely audible.

"That's the point, isn't it?" Fletch asked. "They weren't your brother's ashes. They weren't anybody's ashes. They were just ashes."

"What? How can anybody tell the difference between one person's ashes and another person's ashes? You just tell me that! So a mortuary mixed up ashes. Do you have to tell us that?"

"These aren't human ashes at all, Francine. It isn't a case of a mortuary mixing up ashes. It's a case of your sister-in-law saying, These are human ashes, These are Tom's ashes—when they aren't."

"Then what are they the ashes of?"

"Carpet," said Fletch. "A tightly-woven carpet. Some pine wood. Some sand. A petroleum product, probably kerosene."

Francine put her coffee cup and saucer on the coffee table so forcefully the saucer shattered and the cup fell over.

"I can't stand any more of this."

"Francine, you just told me that when you and Enid arrived in Switzerland last November, Enid collected the ashes from the mortuary. You did not go with her. She arrived back at your hotel carrying ashes she said were Tom's."

"Did I say that?"

"Is it the truth?"

"You have me so confused."

"Enid brought the ashes of her Persian carpet to Switzerland with her."

In the dim light of the livingroom, Francine's eye sockets seemed hollow. The violin music from the wall-speakers was grating on Fletch's ears.

"Listen, Francine." Fletch sat forward and spoke reasonably, quietly into Francine's white, slack face. "Enid told you your brother was dead. Her saying so is the only evidence you have that he's dead. At her suggestion that news of Tom's death would make the running of Wagnall-Phipps impossible for her, you did not rush off to Switzerland. You waited six months. You did not see your brother's body. From what you just said about your trip to Switzerland with Enid, you did not talk with Tom's doctors, or with the undertaker. The United States

Embassy in Switzerland says that no American citizen named Thomas Bradley has died in Switzerland in recent years. The ashes on the mantelpiece in your brother's home in Southworth are not your brother's ashes."

Fletch waited a long moment. Francine's chin looked pinched. Then he took her hand.

"Listen, Francine. It wasn't a happy marriage. I spoke with a neighbor of theirs, in Southworth. He didn't seem your typical neighborhood gossip. But he said he and his wife used to hear Enid screaming all night, doors slamming, things breaking. Not just once in a while, but all the time. While this would be going on, the kids used to roar off in their cars in the middle of the night."

"This is impossible."

"I don't know whether your brother was genuinely sick. Maybe you do?"

"He was."

"Enid might consider herself well off without Tom, especially if she can get you to come run the business."

"You think Enid killed Tom." Francine's statement landed between them like a thrown rock. She withdrew her hand.

Fletch said, "Tell me what else to think."

"I think all this is unnecessary." Francine got up from her chair and strode firmly across the room. She opened the door of a wall cabinet and threw a switch and the music went off. Then she turned a three-way lamp to its brightest. "I think you've assaulted me enough, Irwin Fletcher."

"Assaulted?"

Across the room, standing next to the bright lamp, her dinner dress wrinkled, her hair needing a combing, for the first time in Fletch's eyes, Francine Bradley looked small, vulnerable.

"You've assaulted me and Enid. Over nothing at all."

"I wouldn't call the evidence I've presented 'nothing at all'. I'd call it pretty indicative."

"There's no evidence at all, Fletcher. You're trying to save your job. That's it—pure and simple. I really don't know whether you've made all this up, but you certainly have a motivation to see facts as they aren't. If you don't know it by now, you will by the time you're my age: if you look at any event closely enough, you'll find supposed facts which conflict, contradict what you know to be the truth—memos that are unfiled, or mistakenly initialed, records lost in a bureaucracy—"

"Carpet ashes in a funeral urn?"

"God! It was six months later when we went to Switzerland! How do we know what some obscure Swiss undertaker did? He'd never expect the ashes he gave Enid to be analysed."

"I suspect he could have supplied human ashes—if a Swiss undertaker was the source of the ashes, that is. We all have our pride."

She turned her side to him. "Fletcher, I just can't stand any more of this. Not tonight. I understand that something happened in my brother's company which caused you to lose your job, and that that Charles Blaine has filled you up with all sorts of nonsense. I've tried to be nice, and open with you, and answer your questions." Even with her back to the light, Fletch could see Francine was crying. "And I do appreciate your concern for young Tom, and Ta-ta, and telling me about them. I believe that part. But when you say Enid murdered

Tom! I've never heard anything so insane in my life! It's just too much, too...too insane!"

He stood up and put on his jacket. "Will you at least think about it?"

She looked at him through wet, blinking eyes. "Do you think I'll be able to think about anything else?"

"I'm just asking you to think about it. You've underestimated another woman, Francine. You're being had."

She opened the apartment door. "Good night, Fletch." Her red-rimmed eyes pleaded with him. "Would asking you to go away and leave us alone do any good?"

Fletch kissed Francine Bradley on the cheek. "Good night, Francine. Thanks for dinner."

32

"Good morning, Moxie. Did I wake you up?"

"Of course you woke me up. Who is this?"

"Your landlord. Your banker."

"Jeez, Fletcher, it's Saturday. I don't have to be at rehearsal until two o'clock."

"California time or New York time?"

"Are you still in New York?"

"Yeah, but I'm leaving for Texas in a few minutes."

"Why are you going to Texas?"

"I'm looking for a body, old dear. I keep not finding one."

"Thomas Bradley is not alive and hiding out in New York?"

"Apparently not. Despite my best efforts to shake up his sister, she does not produce him."

"What does she say?"

"She seems genuinely upset by everything I

tell her. She's a smart, cool, efficient lady. She has to know that sooner or later I'm going to blow a whistle, bring what evidence I have to the authorities. I really believe she would produce her brother by now—if it were possible."

"Gee,whiz, Fletch, I have an idea—maybe Thomas Bradley died, despite that article in the *News-Tribune*. Did you ever think of that?"

"I'm beginning to believe in my own theories."

"Oh, no."

"Oh, yes."

"So far, Fletch, darling, your theories have been worth about as much as a grin in a wrestling match."

"Trial and error, trial and error."

"What's in Texas?"

"Everything, if you ask a Texan. It's the original home of the Bradley family."

"So what, she said, eager to roll over and go back to sleep."

"So when you're looking for someone, dead or alive, don't you look in his home?"

"Not nowadays. We don't have homes anymore. Just places where we live. The truth is, Fletch, you have no idea what you're doing."

"You are correct."

"You are spinning your wheels and going nowhere."

"Correct again."

"You're dashing from Mexico to New York to Texas to God-knows-where because way down in your conceited little heart you just can't believe you did the utterly stupid thing of publicly quoting a dead man as if he were still among the quick."

"Your exactitude, Moxie, is doing nothing to encourage me."

"I hope. It's also correct you wouldn't be zipping around the landscape like a bitch in heat if you hadn't received a legacy from one unknowing James St. E. Crandall, and, I might add, my permission to use it."

"Too, true."

"Foolish me."

"I hope you're contrite."

"I'm not contrite. I'm cold in bed alone. A different emotion altogether."

"You should be with me, in an overheated New York hotel room. Steam heat and mirrors everywhere."

"Well, I hope you're having a nice vacation with yourself. If you care, you've lost another job."

"Didn't have another job."

"You did, too. I told you so. The male lead in *In Love.*"

"I've lost that job? Oh, woe is me! Woe! I say, woe!"

"Sam is gone. Replaced by Rick Caswell. He's absolutely marvelous."

"I'm so glad."

"He's physically beautiful, with big lashes, you know?"

"No."

"His timing is perfect."

"No trouble with thick thighs, eh?"

"What? Oh, no. Ran cross-country for Nebraska. He's beautiful."

"I think you said that."

"Did I? Sorry. He's beautiful."

"Oh."

"Really."

"I've got the point. Say, Moxie—?"

"May I go back to sleep now? I mean, I only answered the phone hoping it was your ex-wife again, so I could tell her more lies."

"How'd you like to do some spade work for me?"

"On this Bradley thing?"

"I know you don't believe in it; you're willing to chalk the whole thing up to my own incompetence and stupidity..."

"I really don't have much time, Fletch. The play is opening—"

"Just a little spade work, Moxie."

"Anything, darling. Oh, landlord and banker."

"Would you get a gang together—maybe your pals from the theater—and go dig up Enid Bradley's backyard? She's gone pretty regularly from nine-to-five."

"What?"

"You can tell them it's a treasure hunt, or something."

"Is that what you mean by spade work?"

"You'll want to bring more than one spade, to get the whole yard dug up in eight hours."

"Now you want to help Enid Bradley do her gardening?"

"No, no. You don't get the point. I'm looking for something."

"What?"

"What I'm always looking for: Thomas Bradley."

"What? Fletch, you're not serious!"

"I think Enid planted her husband in the back yard."

"Fletch."

"Yes."

"Fletch, you're not thinking."

"I'm not?"

"If you find Thomas Bradley under his wife's rhododendrons, you'd be proving that he is dead."

"It would strongly so indicate."

"And if Thomas Bradley is dead, you're ruined."

"That certainly has occurred to me."

"So why do you, of all people, want to find his body?"

"Two reasons. It would satisfy my curiosity."

"You have an expensive curiosity. What's your second brilliant reason?"

"It would be a helluva story, of course."

"Fletcher—"

"Will you do it?"

"No."

"You all need the exercise by now. Especially that Rick fellow. Think of spending a nice day digging in the garden."

"Rick does not need the exercise. He's—"

"I know."

"—beautiful."

"Moxie, you make up the damndest, most unacceptable reasons for not doing as you're asked."

"You just don't know how to take being fired gracefully! Roll over, Fletch! Play dead!"

"I'm on to something here, Moxie. I really am. Go dig up the garden. Please!"

"Bye, Fletcher. I just fell back to sleep."

"Moxie? ... Moxie? ... Moxie?"

33

Finally a taxi rolled up to the curb in front of the Dallas Registry. The driver rolled down his window.

"Three forty nine Grantchester Street," Fletch said.

"Why would you want to go there?" The expression on the taxi driver's face was the one taxi drivers all over the world use while talking to *damned furriners who don't know what they're talkin' about.*

"Why wouldn't I want to go there?"

"You lookin' for somebody?"

"You might just say so," Fletch drawled.

"Well, you won't find him."

"I'm beginning to get that idea."

"I'm pretty sure all that way's a big owell."

"A big what?"

" 'Course not sure of that number in particular. What'd you say the number is?"

"Three forty nine."

"Might's well get in. You look more like you can stand to lose the fare'n I can."

Inside his clothes Fletch's body was running with sweat from the dry heat. After he closed the door of the back seat he heard the air conditioner whirring high. The interior of the car was degrees colder. The driver started the car and, not interfering with anyone in Dallas who wanted to get ahead of him, followed the traffic sedately. As he drove he rolled up his window, making the interior of the car even colder.

"All that way's up there a big owell."

At nine o'clock Monday morning Fletch had been at the Registry of Births and Deaths in downtown Dallas, Texas. A slim, gray-haired woman had taken his simple enquiry not only as a great interest and cause of her own but also as an opportunity to be hospitable to someone clearly not native Texan. She poured Fletch coffee from the office pot, offered him a doughnut, which she insisted had been ordered by mistake, disappeared into the stacks and returned with a volume really too big for her to carry and dusty enough to make her white blouse look like it had been run over by a bus. Besides the date of birth, she established that Thomas Bradley indeed had been born in Dallas, Texas, at the Dallas Hospital, of Lucy Jane (McNamara) and John Joseph Bradley, of three forty nine Grantchester Street.

"I'm just tellin' you it's a big owell, sonny, so when we get that way you won't turn on me mad for bringin' you that way."

"I won't turn mad," Fletch promised.

" 'Less you're in 'struction."

"In what?"

"You looked like you're in 'struction I never would say nothin'. But you don't."

"Oh, yes," Fletch said.

The sunlight reflected from a million mirrors as they drove along, from the windows of buildings, the windshields and chromium of cars. The driver was wearing sunglasses.

The sweat on Fletch's body froze. He held his arms close to his body.

The lady at the Registry of Births and Deaths had been very kind and very helpful, dragging out volume after volume for him. He doubted her blouse would ever be pure white again.

The taxi driver took a right turn, then another. The sign saying *Grantchester* was tipped.

Ahead of them, both sides of the street, was an enormous construction site. Chain-link fence ran along both sidewalks. An idle bulldozer dozed among the rubble. There were no workers in sight. Whatever buildings, houses, trees which had been there had been knocked down. On neither side of the road had new building commenced.

"Urban removal," the driver said. He slowed the car and brought it nearer the dusty curb. "A big owell."

"Oh," Fletch said. He had never gone so far to see a hole. "A neighborhood gone."

"No one here," the driver said simply. "Whoever you're lookin' for."

"Guess not."

"No one even to ask after him."

"No."

"Lotsa 'struction goin' on in Dallas," the driver said.

"Makes you proud, don't it?" Fletch said.

He gave the driver the name of the hotel where he had spent Sunday night and would not spend Monday night.

"Francine?"

Fletch had not been sure she would pick up the phone to him. He had identified himself properly to her secretary.

Returning to the hotel he had showered, changed to trunks, played around the hotel's rooftop pool awhile, until he felt his Puerto de San Orlando sunburn beginning to sting again. Now he was sitting on the edge of his bed, wondering which way to dress before checking out.

"Yes, Mister Fletcher. I mean, Fletch." Francine's voice was low, sounded cautious and tired.

"Any new thoughts?" Fletch asked. He had direct-dialled station-to-station. There was no way either the secretary or Francine could know he was calling New York from Dallas.

"About what?"

"About what we talked about Friday night."

"Well, I see that you've been damaged, Fletch. I understand that. Some mix-up at Wagnall-Phipps caused you to lose your job. Your profession. I'd like to talk to Enid about making it up to you."

"How do you mean?"

"Financially. Whether it was Charles Blaine's mistake, or some office mischief—or because of Enid's and my decision to delay news of Tom's death six months—the fact remains you got caught in the middle and suffered damage. It's partly our fault—I see that—or the fault of Wagnall-Phipps. You've suffered damage at our hands. So much so that you're imagining things. Wild things."

Her throaty voice was so soft Fletch realized he was pressing the phone receiver hard against his ear.

"I'd like to recommend to Enid we make it up to you somehow—like give you half a year's pay. Enough to let you go to Europe, or whatever, take a vacation, think out what you're going to do next with your life."

"That's kind of you," he said.

"Well, I really believe we owe it to you. I figure all this confusion happened just to protect Enid's authority in the company, get her through a bad time. There's no reason you should be wiped out by it."

"Francine, where were you born?"

There was a silence before she said, "My father, you know, was an engineer. I was born on station."

"Where was that?"

"Juneau, Alaska."

"I see."

"Fletch, why don't you let me talk to Enid about all this?"

"You don't seem to have thought much of the evidence I presented you, Francine."

"Oh, I've thought about it. And I find simple explanations, for everything, incredibly obvious. The one thing I will never tell Enid about, though, is that that Swiss undertaker gave her the ashes of a burned rug, or whatever you said. That's horrid. I trust you'll never let Enid know, either."

Looking at his toes, Fletch smiled.

"May I see you again?" Fletch asked.

"I wish you would. Toward the end of the week?"

"Thursday night?" Fletch asked.

"Yes. Come to the apartment Thursday evening. By then I'll have talked with Enid at length about all this. I will know what she thinks. I'm sure she'll agree with me. A trip abroad might be nice for you, at this point in your life. Help you sort things out."

Fletch said, "I'll see you Thursday night."

After putting the telephone receiver back in its cradle, Fletch walked across his Dallas hotel room to his suitcase and pulled out his sweater.

34

"Moxie?"

"Fletch?"

"Hello."

"Hey, we're running through the last scene. Someone said I had a call from Juneau, Alaska, for Pete's sake. I don't know anyone in Juneau, Alaska."

"You know me."

"You're in Juneau, Alaska?"

"Yup."

"Boy, you can't do anything right. You aim for Dallas, Texas and hit Juneau, Alaska. Fletch style. Linda warned me about you coming home from the office by way of Hawaii. At least she had a meatloaf to keep her company."

"Stop a minute."

"Are there dead people in Juneau, or what?"

"I was in Dallas yesterday."

"Hey, Fletch. You're not supposed to interrupt rehearsals, you know? I mean, suppose everybody got called to the phone. Opening night would never happen."

"So why did you come to the phone?"

"Thought it might be dear old Freddy calling, demanding the presence of Ophelia again, or something. A lady with nerves of steel for his hard-times knife-throwing act."

"I want to ask you something."

"What? I've got to go back to rehearsal."

"Have you ever been confronted with something you absolutely cannot understand?"

"Sure. My father."

"I mean something which you just can't put your mind around?"

"Sure. My father."

"Where all the facts add up to something which simply isn't possible?"

"Sure. My father."

"I'm serious."

"So am I."

"I'm real serious, Moxie. When you prove out something which absolutely cannot be true?"

"No. I guess not."

"If you were in such a situation, what would you do?"

"Be very suspicious of my conclusion."

"Yeah. I've tried that."

"Doesn't work?"

"No."

"Well, I've got to go back to work."

"I have another question."

"What? When will you be home?"

"Maybe Friday night."

"What's your question?"

"How's Rick?"

"Oh, he's—"

"I know. Bye, Moxie."

35

Before dawn Thursday morning, Fletch was waiting across the street from Francine Bradley's New York apartment house. It was a warm spring morning but he wore his raincoat, his hat. He also wore his clear glasses. He stood in the doorway of a dry cleaning store which had not yet opened. He was surprised to hear the sound of birds in New York City. As dawn broke, he could hear but still not see them. And, of course, he could hear the sirens. Standing anywhere in New York City, anytime, day or night, one can hear a siren from somewhere.

At a quarter to six a taxi cab pulled up in front of Francine's apartment house. Briskly, dressed in a short raincoat and high boots, she left the building and got into the cab.

The taxi was several blocks away, on its way uptown, before Fletch was able to get his own cab.

Traffic was light and it was easy to catch up. Fletch told the driver that in the other cab was his wife, who had forgotten her wallet.

They crossed Central Park at fairly high speed and again turned north.

Francine was let out at the corner of West 89th Street.

Fletch let his cab go and walked slowly to the corner. As he arrived at the corner, he saw Francine enter an alley halfway down the block.

Strolling with his head down, he walked past the mouth of the alley, glancing in. What he saw was an oddity in New York—a cobblestoned stableyard, complete with box stalls, a horse's head above each half-door but one, bales of hay stacked in the corners of the yard. Three grooms were moving around, doing their morning chores. One groom was helping Francine mount a dappled gray.

Fletch continued walking. By the time he reached the end of that block he heard the clatter of hooves on a hard surface, and looked back.

Francine rode out of the alley and turned toward the park. She had removed her short raincoat.

36

"Hi," she said, opening the door of apartment 21M to him.

Fletch looked at Francine's breasts.

It was just after six in the evening and the doorman had said Fletch was expected. The doorman would call Ms. Bradley to say Fletch was on his way up.

"Hi."

Francine Bradley's face had been freshly made up. She wore a pearl necklace. Her cocktail dress was a soft gray, cut low in front. Francine Bradley's breasts were not large but appeared firm for a woman of her age, and, from the cut of her dress, Fletch surmised Francine Bradley was proud of her breasts.

"You look a little tired," she said, closing the door behind him. "New York City life too much for my orange-juice-and-cereal innocent?"

"I've been visiting the suburbs," he said.

She led the way into the livingroom but stopped near the liquor cabinet. He continued on to the far side of the room, to the big window, and looked down. Then he looked out the window.

"Would you like a drink?" she asked.

"Not just yet."

"I guess I'll wait, too."

Francine sat on the divan. "You do seem tired." She resettled a throw-pillow. "A little stiff, too."

"No," Fletch said from the window. "I'm not stiff."

"I daresay you're eager to hear our decision."

"What decision?"

"I've had two or three long talks with Enid. Of course, I never told her all your crazy notions. I told her you'd turned up here and seemed distraught. I took you to dinner and heard you out. It was my understanding you lost your job, really, only because she and I deliberately had delayed news of Tom's death, until Enid had become more established at Wagnall-Phipps. You got caught up in the middle somehow, what with Charles Blaine's craziness and all. In fact, I told Enid you are more or less ruined in your profession—for life. Is that more or less correct?"

"More or less."

"She said you'd been round to the Southworth Prep School, annoying Roberta. She didn't seem to know you'd seen Tom. I told her you'd gone to see both of them, just to apologize. That's true, isn't it?"

"More or less."

"Enid finally came to understand that we're at least partly to blame for what happened to you.

She came to my way of thinking, and agreed we should help you out. I mean, financially."

On a roof across the street Fletch could see an older man and woman sitting in garden chairs under a parasol. A martini shaker and a plate of crackers and cheese were on a small metal table between them. A newspaper lay at the man's feet. As he watched, the woman said something that made the man laugh.

"Of course, we don't know precisely what a reporter earns," Francine continued. "But we figure it will take a good half-year for you to straighten out your life again, find a new interest, a new profession. To calm down and get over this obsession about us. Maybe travelling for a while would help. You could even use what we give you to go back to school."

Fletch heard Francine take a deep breath.

"Of course, for my part, I'm grateful to you for telling me about Tom. We had no idea. Enid has gone to his rooms at college and discovered the sad truth about him. He was dozing in the bathtub—just as you said. Quite given up on life. Enid lost no time in putting him in the hands of experts. Of course it will take a while," she said softly, "but he'll be all right. If nothing else you've done or said makes any sense, Fletch, your making us realize the state Tom was in leaves us entirely in your debt. But that's a human thing..."

Her voice trailed off.

On the roof across the street the man was pouring the woman another martini.

"So." Francine's voice brightened. "Enid and I have decided to try to make things up to you by giving you half a year's pay. We'll arrange it through

Wagnall-Phipps somehow, so it won't cost us so much. To do with as you like, go where you like. Give you a chance to straighten out your own life."

"No."

"What?"

Fletch continued to look through the window. "No."

"Really," Francine said after a moment. "Isn't that really why you went to see Enid, and came to see me, Fletch? You felt we owed you something? Be honest with yourself. Weren't you really hoping we'd have some understanding of what you're going through, and, shall we say, help you out?"

"No."

"What's wrong? Aren't we offering you enough? You do want our financial help, don't you?"

"No."

There was a long silence in the darkening room.

Fletch watched the older couple across the street fold up their garden chairs, gather up their newspaper, martini pitcher, glasses, plate of crackers and cheese, and disappear through the roof hatch.

37

Fletch said, "I'm sure Melanie is looking forward to your reincarnation."

He turned from the window in time to see Francine's hands flutter, her effort to keep surprise, alarm from her face. Her final expression was patronizing. "Now what are you talking about?"

"Melanie. Your horse. Your horse in California. No one ever sold your horse."

"What do you mean, *my horse?*"

"I don't get this even slightly." Standing in front of the window, Fletch shrugged. "You're Tom Bradley."

"My God!" Francine said. "Now the man has totally flipped!"

His face screwed in perplexity, again he looked at her breasts. "Maybe."

"First you told me Enid murdered Tom, and now you're telling me I am Tom!" Her laugh came entirely from her throat. "Maybe you do need more than half-a-year off!"

Fletch, with the light of the window behind him, peered at her on the divan. "I must say," he said, "you're marvelous."

"Enid hasn't sold Tom's horse—Melanie, or whatever her name is—*ergo* I'm my brother? Enid's been busy, you know—very busy. She's been running a family, and a good-sized company. Selling a horse is the last thing she has to worry about."

"You ride horseback," Fletch said. "I watched you this morning, on West 89th Street."

"Yes, I enjoy riding. My brother enjoyed riding. Does that make me my brother?"

"The night we had dinner," Fletch said, "last Friday night, you spent almost the entire time telling me a long, convoluted, not-very-funny barnyard story."

"So what? I'm sorry if you didn't like my story. I'd had a drink. I thought it was funny."

"Long, not-very-funny dirty jokes are characteristic of Thomas Bradley. As reported to me by Mabel Franscatti, Alex Corcoran, Mary Blaine and Charles Blaine."

"Tom and I had certain characteristics in common. We're brother and sister. Fletch, are you insane?"

"Brother...sister. You are your brother."

"I'm also my own grandfather."

"Could be."

"What's the point of this joke?"

"The point is I have only one piece of paper, when I should have, by this time, three pieces of paper." He took from his inside jacket pocket Thomas Bradley's birth certificate and placed it on the coffee table in front of her. "Thomas Bradley was born in Dallas, Texas."

She nodded. "Thank you. I knew that."

"I went to Dallas, Sunday," he said. "By the way, your old neighborhood's torn down."

She shrugged. "There goes the neighborhood."

"You were not born in Dallas, Texas."

"I told you. I was born in Juneau, Alaska."

"Tuesday I was in Juneau, Alaska. You were not born in Juneau, Alaska."

Francine stared at him.

"And Thomas Bradley did not die in Switzerland." Fletch had returned to stand by the window, but he was still watching her. "So, instead of having two birth certificates and one death certificate, I've got only one birth certificate. And that's your's. The Bradleys had only one child—a son named Thomas."

"I was born well outside Juneau, about a hundred miles—"

"You weren't born at all, Francine."

She sighed and looked away. "My God."

"And Tom Bradley didn't die."

"You do believe in pieces of paper, Fletcher. Bureaucracies, clerks, secretaries—"

"And Swiss undertakers. I believe in Swiss undertakers. You've been writing those memos to Accounting yourself, Francine, and initialing them 'T.B.', probably without even realizing you were doing it. We all have low-level habits that are just second-nature to us. We all do certain things in certain ways, and we continue doing them, under all circumstances, unconsciously." Looking at her, he gave her a moment. "True?"

"No," she said.

"Francine, would you come here, please?"

She looked a scared, unwilling child.

"Please come here," he said.

She rose and came across the room to him unsteadily, leaving the low table between them.

"Look down," he said.

She looked at the tile mosaic on the low table.

"Almost finished, isn't it?" he asked.

"Yes."

"When I first entered your apartment, a week ago, it was less than half finished."

Looking down at the mosaic, her mouth opened slowly.

"I see."

"Come on, Tom," Fletch said. "I'm not trying to embarrass anybody. As you said, I'm just trying to save my own ass."

Francine cupped a hand to her face, bridging cheekbone and forehead, turned, and started across the livingroom toward the foyer. She bumped into a free-standing chair.

Fletch heard her high heels click across the foyer's hardwood floor. And then he heard her knock on a door.

"Enid?" she called. "Enid, would you please come help me, dear?"

38

"Fletch, do you believe in the soul?"

"The soul is immaterial," he said.

Francine asked, "Is that meant as a pun?"

"Of course."

Enid Bradley had entered the livingroom from the foyer, putting one sensible shoe unsteadily ahead of the other as if unsure of where she was going. "Hello, Mrs. Bradley," Fletch had said. She looked worried, confused, and said nothing.

Francine entered more briskly behind her, and took her by the arm. Together they sat on the divan.

Fletch loosened his tie and collar and sat on the freestanding chair. "Sorry," he said. Again he looked at Francine's breasts. "I just don't understand." Seeing the two of them together he realized Francine was the shorter. In the photograph behind him, Thomas Bradley was shorter than his wife. "And I need to understand. I have to save myself."

Each woman had her hands in her own lap. Francine sat the straighter. *Enid always looks terrified of what the next moment will bring—you know, as if she's afraid someone is going to say something dirty,* Mary Blaine had said that night in Puerto de San Orlando. *Her husband usually does,* Charles Blaine had answered. *I mean, did.*

"Fletch," Francine asked. "Do you know what a transsexual is?"

"I can't say I understand. I'd like to be able to say I do."

You can't understand everything that happens, Roberta, Ta-ta, had said jogging through the California woods... *You can try to understand, of course. You can even act like you understand, when you don't yet. But some things...*

"A male can be born in a female body," Francine said simply. "Or a female born in a male body."

"What defines us as male or female, except our bodies?" Fletch asked.

"Our souls," Francine said. "To use your word, there is an immaterial self independent of the material self—our bodies. I was a female born in a male's body. That's all there is to it. I've known it since I was two or three years old. As long as I can remember I had feminine desires. A great interest in feminine clothes. I had a feminine perspective on everything. I liked dolls and babies and pretend tea parties and having my hair done up. I remember the first time my father introduced me as *his son, Tom,* I stared at him in shock. I was a girl. That was all there was to it. I knew I was a girl."

Francine went to the bar and began to pour out three Scotch and waters.

"I went through high school, as a boy, in Dallas, Texas. I wore trousers and sweat shirts and played on the varsity baseball team. I wasn't a bad short stop. Gee, you know, I almost just said I could throw like a boy." She smiled at Fletch. "I dated girls and was elected treasurer of my senior class. I became a superb actor. With every word, every expression on my face, I acted the complete male. I was the complete male. I had the equipment, and I could get it up on demand. Don't ask me what I was really thinking, in the back seat with Lucy, or Janey, or Alice. Girls loved me especially because I understood them so well. All through college—boys' dormitories, boys' fraternity houses, well, all that was sort of nice. But I felt a cheater—because I was a girl."

She brought Fletch's drink to him.

"Can you imagine a worse conflict than being a girl in a boy's body? Or a woman in a man's body? No life can be worse than the life which obliges you to be dishonest with every word, every expression, in every living moment."

She took the two remaining drinks from the bar to the divan, and, sitting down, handed one to Enid, who drained half of it immediately.

To Fletch, Francine said, "You repeated to me that some nosy neighbor of our's in Southworth told you he could hear Enid screaming and shrieking at night. That wasn't Enid. That was me—Tom Bradley—shrieking to get out of my body." Francine tasted her drink. "Then came the Sunday morning that I swallowed everything in the medicine cabinet. I would rather have died than continue this lie, this life, this act, the agony of this conflict within myself." Francine's free hand took Enid's free hand and held it. "Enid promised to help me make the change. Enid is my dearest friend and greatest love."

Fletch asked Enid, "You knew about this before?"

"Of course," Enid said.

"For years?"

"Yes."

"It's something a husband really can't conceal from a wife," Francine said, "for long. I married thinking I could carry it off, carry on the act forever. But I couldn't. You see, Fletch, a person like me has the suspicion that every male—even you—would rather be a female. I know it's not true. I just don't see why you'd want to be a male."

"Why did you get married?" Fletch asked.

"Because," Francine said, "I had a very strong maternal instinct. It was my only way of having babies. Can you understand that? Also I loved Enid, very much." She continued to hold Enid's hand. "I won't ask you to understand that."

"Are Roberta and Tom your own children?"

"Of course." Francine smiled. "I told you. I was fully equipped. There was no reason why I shouldn't have children—as a father."

Fletch said, "Wow."

Francine smiled. "Do you need a moment to catch up?"

"Enid," Fletch said, "I thought you'd murdered him."

"I murdered myself," Francine said, "in the only way I could stay alive. Sometimes, young

Fletch, we must do radical things to keep on living."

Again Fletch found himself staring at Francine's breasts.

"Yes," Francine said, "for two years before the surgical transformation began, I took hormonal shots. They softened my body, changed the shape of it, enlarged my breasts." *The only comment I made about it to my wife was that he seemed to be getting smaller,* Alex Corcoran had said in the golf club bar. "I also underwent two years of intensive psychotherapy, to make sure this was the right thing for me."

The room was growing entirely dark. No one moved to turn on a light.

"Surgery?" Fletch asked.

"Yes," Francine said. "Surgery."

Fletch remembered the motion Tom, Jr. had made sitting in his bathtub, of sticking a knife into the lower part of his own stomach, and rooting it around there.

"I still have one more operation," Francine said happily. "Then I can go home again."

"As Francine Bradley."

"Yes. As Francine. I can carry it off. You see, after all these years of acting, I'm not acting anymore. I really am Francine Bradley. I never was Tom."

"You convinced me."

"Enid and I carefully built the myth, over time, that there was a Francine. Tom's sister. Smart, competent at business, knew everything there was to know about Wagnall-Phipps. Would take it over, if ever anything happened to Tom."

"Your children—Ta-ta and Tom—they know the truth, don't they?"

"Yes," Francine said. "We thought they were old enough. They had seen enough of my pain, my agony. I guess Tom wasn't quite old enough. Of course, this sort of thing is much harder on fathers and sons than on daughters. Ta-ta can understand my transforming myself into a woman, because she is one. We sincerely did not know, Fletch, until you told me, how much trouble Tom was in. He has to make his own life, you know. I have to make mine."

Fletch realized he had been drinking his Scotch absently. It was gone. "And you just kept writing those memos to Blaine, and initialing them 'T.B.' without even knowing you were doing it."

Through the dark, he heard Francine sigh. "In a way, that's the worst part of a transformation like this. The little things. Changing the name on bank accounts, credit cards, Social Security. There's always one more thing—something you forget. It would be easier if one did die and go through probate. A few months ago I got stopped for speeding on the Connecticut Throughway. There I was, a blonde, middle-aged female, in a cocktail dress and high heels, driving on the California license of Thomas Bradley. Half my identification said I was Francine, half Thomas. The policeman was deeply perplexed, poor man. He took me to the police station. I told them the truth. Do you know, they understood it. It took them awhile, but they were really very understanding and respectful. Well, they have to be now. There are thousands of us in the United States now. Thank God, we haven't become a statistic yet. We're still too much under-the-rug. But we exist. By the way, I still got that ticket for speeding. In the name of Francine." She laughed. "I paid the fine, gladly. I love anything that tells me I'm Francine. I'm finally Francine! Of course," she said more seriously, "getting a speeding ticket in Connecticut isn't the same as having you expose me in the newspaper."

Quietly, Fletch said, "I think you'd better tell Charles Blaine about this."

"Oh, no," Francine said. "How would Charley ever understand? He's so straight, so literal."

"He and Mary are more understanding than you think," Fletch said. "They have a good influence on them—her aunt."

"Oh, yes. Happy," Francine said. "How I used to hate that woman. She is so much a woman, and so happy at being a woman, being alive. I guess I don't have to hate her anymore."

In the dark, Enid blurted, "What are you going to do?"

"Me?" Fletch asked.

"We didn't murder anyone," Enid said. "All we did is lie. Are you going to ruin us, ruin the company, because we lied? We have a right to privacy, you know. Francine has a right to live her life in the only way possible for her."

More calmly, Francine said, "Forgive us our elaborate lies, Fletch. But you know the world isn't ready for this. It would hurt the company. I'd be seen as a freak. Key people would quit the company. Alex Corcoran wouldn't be able to sell a fire extinguisher to someone on his way to hell."

"Are you going to write about us in the newspaper?" Enid's voice was ready to sob.

"I'd like to tell my managing editor about all this," Fletch said. "I'd like my job back."

"He'll print it, for sure!" said Enid.

"No, no," Fletch said. "A newspaper knows a lot of stories it doesn't print. There's one now Frank Jaffe is sitting on, about where the state police used to get their police cars. This story, especially, is not in the public interest. Tom's becoming Francine is nobody's business but Francine's."

Francine snapped on the light beside the divan. Her face was charming, smiling. She said, "We never expected you to have so much persistance, Fletch. Mexico, New York, Dallas, Juneau, back here—phew!"

"We never thought you could afford it," Enid said. She was almost smiling.

"I couldn't," Fletch said. "I—uh—sort of borrowed the money."

Francine got up and took her glass to the bar. "Can we make it up to you?"

"I think I'll be all right."

"Francine, dear." Enid held up her empty glass. "My glass has been empty a long time."

Laughing, Francine came over and collected Enid's and Fletch's glasses, taking them to the bar.

"That was your mistake, in fact," Fletch said.

"What was?" Francine asked indifferently.

Fletch said to Enid, "When I went to your house, essentially you offered me money. Never offer a reporter money."

"Or what?" Francine asked from the bar.

"Or he'll sink his teeth into you," Fletch said. "And never let go."

39

"Thomas Bradley is not dead," Fletch said, walking into Frank Jaffe's office. "He is alive and living in New York city in a different *persona*. Essentially, he is running Wagnall-Phipps. He did write and initial those memos. I quoted him fairly and accurately. I want my job back."

There had been boos and catcalls as Fletch walked across the City Room of the *News-Tribune* Friday afternoon. Someone had shouted, "Hey, there's Fletch! Back from the dead! Again!" Others had been silent and looked away.

"Janey," Fletch said in the managing editor's outer office, "Frank in?"

"Yes, he is," she said. "Why are you?"

"Please tell him I'm here with something important to tell him."

"What do you have to tell him?"

"It's unprintable."

Fletch was made to wait in Frank Jaffe's outer office more than an hour. People went by him, in and out of Frank's office. If they knew Fletch, they scowled at him and said nothing—all but one old reporter, whose look and nod were friendly. He said, "Hi, Fletch."

"Hi."

"You all right?"

"Happy as a baker at breakfast."

"That's good."

Frank Jaffe had looked up from his desk sideways at Fletch when he entered, "It's nice of me to see you."

"Yes, it is," Fletch said, closing the door behind him.

Frank's face remained quizzical through Fletch's statement and demand. Then he snorted.

"It's time I had a little entertainment." Frank looked at his watch. "Late Friday afternoon. You got a story?"

Without being asked, Fletch sat in one of the two chairs facing Frank's desk. While Fletch talked, Frank's eyes wandered behind their permanent film, looked impatient at what appeared to be the prologue to a rather long story, curious when Fletch began mentioning all the airplanes he had been on, intrigued when the facts Fletch recited continued to be contradictory... Fletch told him about meeting the Bradleys, Enid, Roberta, and Tom, Jr., their neighbor, about his friend in the District Attorney's office establishing that Thomas Bradley did not die in Switzerland, that the ashes in his funeral urn were not human ashes, about going to Mexico to interview Mary and Charles Blaine, to New York to interview Francine Bradley, to Dallas, Texas, to Juneau, Alaska, and back to New York...

Frank Jaffe's face colored as Fletch reported his final conversation with Francine Bradley, the night before, in New York, and described Francine and Enid sitting next to each other on the divan, holding hands, being brave in their fear, finally being honest in their difficulty.

"My God," Frank said. "A murder story without a murder. You do come up with some beauts, Fletch. We can't print that."

"Glad to hear you say that. I assured the Bradleys we wouldn't run the story."

" 'We'? Who are 'we'? You still speaking for the *News-Tribune?*"

"Journalistic 'we', Frank. I won't write the story, and you won't run it. Right?"

"Of course not." Frank ran a dry hand over the stubble on his cheeks and jowl. "Not without their permission."

"That you'll never get."

"I suppose not. The Bradleys would lose too much by our running the story. Wagnall-Phipps would dry up faster than a drizzle in Las Vegas. What Tom Bradley—I mean, Francine Bradley has done does not affect the public interest in any way. People have a right to their personal lives."

Frank Jaffe's watery eyes looked long at Fletch. It was clear to Fletch that the managing editor— despite what he said—was tempted by the story. It was also clear to Fletch that Frank Jaffe had every reason to protect people's right to privacy. He wanted his own personal privacy, and privacy for Clara Snow.

Fletch smiled at his managing editor. After a moment, Frank smiled back.

"Helluva story, though," Frank said.

He squared his swivel chair with his desk. "You broke into and entered the Bradley's house? Is that what you said?"

"I didn't break anything. The door to the swimming pool was not locked."

"You broke and entered," Frank said. "Are the Bradleys pressing charges against you?"

"I wasn't stealing human ashes—I was stealing the ashes of a rug."

"What made you so sure they weren't Tom Bradley's ashes?"

"I wasn't sure. I was hoping. What made me do it? All you knew is that I'd said I'd seen memos dated recently and signed 'T.B'. I knew I'd really seen them. Second, of course, Enid Bradley had been quick to offer me money to go away."

"That's the best way to stimulate the curiosity of a good reporter," Frank smiled. "Or corrupt a bad one."

"Honest, Frank, I wasn't sure of myself, even last night, standing in Francine's apartment—until she offered me half-a-year's pay to go away and get off their case. Only then did I decide to blunder ahead."

"You still didn't realize the truth?"

"How could I? Here was a middle-aged woman—I mean, a woman, Frank, a real woman, with breasts—and a missing middle-aged man, father of two children—"

"Ah, the naiveté of the young."

"Would you have known better?"

Frank smiled and nodded his head at the wall. "There's a guy in the City Room whose name used to be Elizabeth."

"You're kidding."

"I'm not kidding. You know him well. The wonders of contemporary science."

Fletch shook his head. "I'm going to give up on my orange juice-and-cereal innocence pretty soon."

"If it weren't for human differences, Fletch, you and I would have nothing to write about." Frank's forearms were on the desk, his hands folded. "By the way, how do I confirm this story of your's? Not that I think you made it up."

"Call Enid Bradley. She and I flew back on the plane together last night. We're friends. You can even call Francine Bradley, in New York."

"I will," Frank said. "I will."

"Frank, do I get my job back?"

"Sure. Report Monday morning."

"And my expenses. I had big expenses sorting this business out, Frank. Will you refund my expenses?"

"No way."

"Why not?"

"No story."

"Jeez, Frank."

"Why should we pay expenses on a story we can't print?"

"At least you're going to refund my last two weeks' pay."

"We are not."

"You're not?"

"The fact remains, Fletch: you goofed. You

were called upon to defend an important element in a story you wrote for this newspaper, and you couldn't defend it right away."

"But I have defended it."

"Two weeks later. And we can't publicly defend your story. The newspaper remains embarrassed. You're lucky to have your job back."

Fletch was standing over the desk. "You mean to say, Frank Jaffe, that in order to write a lousy twelve-paragraph story on a lousy, no-'ccount, two-bit company, for the lousy, gray pages of the Financial Section of the *News-Tribune*, I was supposed to have found out the Chairman of the Board had gone off for sex-change operations?"

"Yep," Frank said. "That's what I mean."

"You know what you're full of, Frank?"

"Lemme see. Do you spell it with four letters?"

"Damnit, Frank!"

"Report Monday," Frank Jaffe said. "And don't ever write anything again you can't defend immediately."

"Blast you, Frank Jaffe."

"Cheers, Fletch."

Amid a widening pool of silence, Fletch sat down at his desk in the City Room. Someone had placed a sign on his desk which read R.I.P.

Fletch took the sign off the desk, and dropped it in the waste basket. Then he smiled at all the other reporters sitting at desks around him.

Al said, loudly enough for everyone around him to hear him, "Finally come to clean out your desk, Fletch?"

"No. I'm not doing that."

"Then what are you doing?"

"Just stopped by to make sure it's still here. I'll need it Monday."

The silence became brittle enough to crack with a hammer. Even the police radios became quiet.

Randall, the religion news reporter said, "You mean, Frank has taken you back? Given you your job back?"

"That's what I mean," Fletch said. "That's exactly what I mean."

Everyone around him exchanged looks—significant looks, angry looks.

"See you Monday," Fletch said, getting up from his desk. "Nice weekend, everybody."

He crossed the City Room. At the door to the foyer, he looked back. What was clearly a delegation of editors and reporters was barging into Frank's office. Clara Snow was in the middle of the pack.

Fletch knew the delegation thought they were going in to protest his rehiring to the managing editor. What they were really doing, being journalists, was going in to get a story—whatever story Fletch had told Frank.

And Fletch knew they would not get the story from Frank.

Laughing, Fletch left the building.

A meter maid was putting a parking ticket on his car.

He took it from her, thanked her, then made her blush by kissing her lightly on the cheek.

40

In the shower, Fletch thought he heard the doorbell ringing, but didn't care much. Then definitely he heard a banging on the front door sufficient to wake the asleep in a burning building.

Having grabbed a towel around him, he opened the front door.

Two men stood in the corridor. One was small and well-dressed and had mean, glinty eyes. The second was large, not well-dressed, and had mean, glinty eyes.

"You have the wrong apartment," Fletch said. "I hope."

"Irwin Maurice Fletcher?"

"Well, as long as you asked." Dimly, Fletch remembered the large man had been in the lobby of the apartment house when Fletch had entered, watched him pick up his mail, and came up in the elevator with him. Vaguely, Fletch had thought he looked like a carnival wrestler with much experience, and wondered if he might not make an interesting interview.

Now he thought avoiding an interview with this man might be the more prudent course.

The small man said, "I'm James St. Eustice Crandall."

"Eustice?"

"You have something that belongs to me."

"I have?" Like tanks the men entered the apartment. Like a wet, near-naked laborer, Fletch backed up before the tanks. "Oh, yes. So I have. Sort of."

"What do you mean, 'sort of'?" the small man asked.

The large man closed the front door.

Fletch hitched his towel firmly around his waist.

"May I see proof you're James St. Eustice Crandall?"

"Sure," the small man said. "Sure. That's reasonable."

He took a driver's licence from his wallet and handed it to Fletch.

Who held it in his hand and stared at it as long as he could.

"What's the matter?" the small man asked.

"I'm sure it's just a bureaucratic error, but your licence says James Reilly."

The small man snatched it from him, stuffed it back into his wallet without glancing at it, took out another licence and shoved it into Fletch's hand.

"Ah!" said Fletch, examining it. "You're James St. E. Crandall, too! I can tell. The pictures match."

He handed the licence back. "It must be nice being a schizocarp. You can scratch your own back."

"Come on," the small man said. "I want my wallet."

"Sure," Fletch said. He stepped back into the livingroom. The large man stepped with him. The large man was keeping Fletch within striking range. "I was wondering how much of a reward you're considering?"

"For what?"

"For finding your wallet and returning it to you."

"You didn't return it to me. I had to come get it."

"I advertised," Fletch said. "Two newspapers."

"Bullshit you did. I didn't see no advertisement."

"Then how did you find me?"

"The San Francisco police. Some hotel manager turned you in. They said you were scarperin' with my dough. They even showed me a picture of you in the newspapers, caught pushin' an old lady off a bridge or somethin'. They said, 'That's the guy'. You, ya punk."

"Oh, boy."

Red appeared around the small man's eyes. "I been waitin' for you all week! Make with the wallet!"

"No reward?"

"Get outta here with that shit!"

"I'd like to." The front door wasn't even visible behind the large man. "I was just thinking a reward of about three thousand, nine hundred and eighty-two dollars might be nice."

"Nice, mice!" The small man put his index finger against Fletch's chest. "Tearin' your skin off in strips would be nice."

"That's the amount I don't have."

The small man eyes popped. "You don't have?"

"I spent it."

"How could you spend my money? Son-of-a-bitch!"

"Something came up, you see. Had to take a jaunt."

The small man shook his head and made every apparent effort to sound reasonable. "Listen, kid, this is my gambling money, got that? Know what that means?"

"Oh, no. Not that syndrome."

"That's my poke. My stake. That's exactly where my winnin's are, in a particular enterprise. I need the whole stake. Intact. Or it's no good for me."

Fletch sighed. "Oh, boy."

"I lost my poke!" the man complained. "In the street somewhere. I can't use no other money in this particular enterprise. Last two weeks, you've cost me a fortune!"

"Oh, yeah," Fletch said.

"Maybe two, three hundred thousand dollars."

"Yeah, yeah. Sure."

"I gotta have every dime of it back! The original money I won!"

Fletch turned more sideways to them, so he would have a back leg to balance a blow. "I haven't got three thousand, nine hundred and eighty-two dollars of it."

"What right you got spending from my poke?"

"None," Fletch admitted.

The small man's little fist hit Fletch hard in the shoulder. The large man did not move. He just continued to pollute the environment with garlicy breath.

"You get my money back! Every damned dime of it! Or Lester here will use your head for a basketball!"

"Lester," Fletch said sincerely, "I believe what the man says."

To the small man, Fletch said, "I think I can make up the money, get it for you. But it will take a while."

The small man threw himself petulantly into a chair. "We'll give you an hour."

"Enid?" Even turned away from Lester, speaking into the phone, Fletch could smell the garlic. "Fletch."

"Hello, Fletch. How's the jet lag? You must feel like a tennis ball at Wimbleton."

"I'm as well as can be expected."

"Your managing editor, Mister Jaffe, called. I told him everything—confidentially, of course."

"Thank you. Listen, do you remember I mentioned to you and Francine that I sort of borrowed money to do all the travelling?"

"Yes."

"Well, the thugs I sort of borrowed it from—" There was suddenly a sharp pain just below Fletch's right rib cage.—I mean the philosophers I took it from are here, wanting it back, right away."

"Fletch, you went to the loan sharks. Oh, dear. You should have said something."

"I'm saying something now."

"How much?"

"Let's phrase it as three thousand, nine hundred and eighty-two dollars in crisp, new one thousand dollar bills. In a big hurry."

"I'll be there as soon as I can. What's your address?"

Fletch told her and then said, "Enid, this isn't blackmail."

"I know that, Fletch. We gave you every opportunity for that. I'll be right there."

After he hung up, rubbing his side, Fletch said, "May I go put some clothes on?"

"No sense in spoiling 'em," the large man said. "They'll just get all bloody, most likely."

"Yeah," said the small man in the armchair. "You might as well leave 'em clean, so someone else can use 'em. Salvation Army."

They waited just over an hour. During that time the large man remained standing over where Fletch sat on the couch.

Lester seemed to have a fascination for Fletch's ears. He kept staring at them. Every time Fletch looked at him, Lester nodded at Fletch's ears and grinned. Obviously Lester's own ears had been maliciously treated. There were teeth marks in them.

Fletch tried to turn his mind to other matters.

On the coffee table, among many bills, was a letter from the Office of The Mayor. It read,

> *Dear Mister Fletcher:*
> *This letter expresses the extreme displeasure of this office, and of The Mayor himself, at your failure to appear to receive your Good Citizenship of the Month Award last Friday morning. The Mayor and*

*the press were looking forward to seeing you. Your
indifferent attitude (you did not even contact this
office ahead of time to notify us of your inability to
appear) has gone a long way toward jeopardizing the
Mayor's entire Good Citizenship of the Month Award
program.*

*The Mayor has directed me to inform you that
your award has been rescinded.*

Sincerely,

The Office of The Mayor

Fletch looked toward his own front door, and
said, in a small voice, "Help! Police!"

Not succeeding in turning his mind to other
matters, Fletch asked the small man, "When I
called you from the lobby of the Park Worth
Hotel, and told you I had your wallet, why didn't
you come right down and take it from me? I
mean, seeing you want it so much?"

"That wasn't you."

"Of course it was me."

"Naw." The small man was definite. "There
was this other guy, see? He knew I had the wallet
with the twenty five grand in it. At that particular
time I owed this other guy considerably more than
the twenty five grand. He was just connin' me, to
get me down into the lobby. I got another friend
to check out for me. I went out the back way."

"But you knew you'd lost your wallet."

"I thought it was in the car. I'd left it under
the car seat. It must have fell out. Or you, or the
other guy stole it."

Fletch sighed. "Now do you know it was me—trying to give you your money back?"

The small man grinned. "I know it wasn't.'

"Why?"

"You find twenty-five grand in cash and try to give it back to me? Come on. You think I'm crazy?"

Fletch reflected a moment, and then said, "You shouldn't ask personal questions."

When the doorbell rang, Lester moved quickly to open the door. He said nothing. Enid's voice said, "Fletch! Are you all right?" Lester slammed the door. When he turned he had four one-thousand dollar bills in his hand.

"Sure!" Fletch yelled. "Thank you!"

"Ugly old broad," Lester said.

The small man had rushed to Lester and grabbed the money. He counted the four bills five times.

"Where's the rest?" he asked Fletch.

Fletch got up and went into the bedroom closet and took the wallet from where he had hidden it in Moxie's purse and brought it back to the livingroom. He tossed it to the small man.

After catching it the small man gave Fletch a look of outrage. His gambling money shouldn't be so desecrated.

And the short man counted the twenty one bills five times. Then he placed the four one thousand dollar bills neatly and smoothly in his wallet, and put the wallet in his jacket pocket.

Before opening the front door, the small man said, "Work him over, Lester. Break his head. All the trouble he's caused me. And four of these bills—" He tapped his wallet through his suit jacket "—just aren't the originals! It will cost me, you bet! You bastard!"

"Lester?" Fletch asked. "Did you hear the one about the near-sighted veterinarian and the garden hose?"

Fletch's observation had been correct: Lester had a fascination for ears. He beat on other parts of Fletch's body as well, but most of those blows were merely intended to get Fletch's forearms down from protecting his head. Lester hit Fletch's left ear repeatedly, then his right ear repeatedly, then alternated between the left ear and the right ear.

The large man might have become bored with his task sooner, if Fletch had not landed a hard one on his nose, making it bleed.

The small man came back, stuck his head through the open front door, and said, "Lester, come on! I've got the elevator waiting."

Wiping his nose on his sleeve, Lester left, closing the front door behind him.

From the floor, which was the only place Fletch had found he could retreat from Lester's final enthusiasm for his job, Fletch heard the men, small and large, walk down the corridor. He heard the elevator door slide shut.

Fletch said, "Finders weepers."

41

The loud ringing in his head took on a slightly different tone, a harmony, once again, so Fletch reasoned the telephone was ringing. Still on the floor, still not breathing evenly, he pulled the telephone cord. It clattered to the floor in two pieces, but Fletch did not hear the clatter. He pulled the two pieces of the telephone to him.

"Hello?" he said into it.

"Oh, Fletch, you are home."

"What about phone?"

"Why are you shouting?"

"Moxie?"

"Fletch, Rick has asked me to move into his pad with him."

"Had with him? Had with who?"

"Stop shouting. It's been damned difficult. I've been spending every damned day and night with him doing this play, and, you know, it's not

Major Barbara we're rehearsing, I mean, Paul has been a complete nut about our getting the nude scenes right, and, frankly, Fletch, Rick is beautiful, and very nice, perfect timing, and how do you expect a girl to take the strain? You haven't been here much, you know."

"How's Rick?"

"Fletch, are you deaf? Why are you breathing hard? Been exercising?"

"When are you coming home?"

"Will you come get me?"

"How could I forget you?"

"I lost the little yellow car that went beep-beep nicely. Parked it in front of the theater and it wasn't there when I came out. I told the police about it, but they didn't seem to much care."

"I'll come pick you up."

"Well, listen, Fletch, are you going to be home from now on? I mean, no girl can take this kind of strain."

"Train? Why take a train? What train? I'll come get you. It will take me a few minutes. I'm in the middle of a shower."

"Oh. That's why you're shouting."

"Hey, Moxie? I got my job back."

"That's wonderful."

"What? Sure. Be right there. Just wait for me."

Fletch hung up the phone, rolled over and sat up. The floor heaved. The walls wobbled. His eyes said they wanted to close. His stomach complained of having nothing to vomit.

He decided he should lie still a moment, on the rug, before washing off the blood, getting dressed, attempting to drive. He rolled over again, slowly, onto his stomach. He put his sore right cheekbone down gently on his sore right forearm.

And fell asleep.